DIPPED IN MURDER

KATHLEEN SUZETTE

❀ Created with Vellum

SIGN UP

Sign up to receive my newsletter for updates on new releases and sales:

https://www.subscribepage.com/kathleen-suzette

Follow me on Facebook:

https://www.facebook.com/Kathleen-Suzette-Kate-Bell-authors-759206390932120

CHAPTER 1

I took a sip of my coffee, a Cherry Mocha Blast, and closed my eyes as the sweet, chocolate and cherry-flavored goodness rolled over my tongue and down my throat, warming me up. "Mmm. This is so good."

My best friend, Lucy Gray, sat across from me at the Cup and Bean coffee shop. She nodded as she took a sip of her own coffee, a raspberry white chocolate mocha. "Mine is really good too. I love the combination of raspberry and white chocolate."

I opened my eyes and looked at her cup. I had had a tough time deciding what I wanted to drink, and I had almost chosen the raspberry white chocolate mocha myself. "I do too. I'll have to try that one next time." I glanced at the coffee shop window and shivered as it began to snow again. It was February in Maine, and we wouldn't see warm weather for at least two months or more. Occasionally, we would experience a false spring, but having lived here as long as I had, I knew that Mother Nature was just toying with us. I turned to Lucy. "Are you and Ed doing anything special for Valentine's Day?"

She snorted, shaking her head. "Me and Ed?" she laughed. "You know how he is. He's as far from romantic as a man can get."

I nodded sympathetically. Sometimes I felt sorry for Lucy because she was right about Ed. The man didn't have a romantic bone in his body. "Why don't you take the initiative? You could plan a romantic dinner or even buy him flowers. Maybe all he needs is to experience the things you enjoy, and he'll reciprocate."

She shook her head. "No, I tried that early in our marriage, but it never worked. He just doesn't care about that kind of thing. It's like he's oblivious to it, even though every store is filled with Valentine's Day reminders. He always seems surprised when the day arrives."

I took another sip of my coffee and sighed. "I'll tell you what, why don't I prepare a nice Valentine's Day dinner at my house? It can be a small celebration for all of us."

One eyebrow shot up. "What? Why would you do that?"

I shrugged. "Because I enjoy cooking, and why not?"

"Well, I appreciate the offer, but you and Alec should go somewhere romantic and enjoy yourselves without us. We'll be fine. Ed may not be traditionally romantic, but I know he loves me. I don't need flowers or candy to prove that."

As much as I wanted to help Lucy, I knew she was right. Ed was never going to change. Besides, Alec probably had plans for us for Valentine's Day. "Suit yourself then. But you do deserve flowers and candy," I insisted.

She nodded. "And that's exactly why I buy them for myself. That way, I get exactly what I want," she declared, tucking a lock of her short pink hair behind her ear. Lucy liked her hair to have some flair, and since we were approaching Valentine's Day, she went with pink.

I chuckled. "Well, that's certainly one approach."

Just then, we were greeted with a blast of cold air as the front door of the coffee shop swung open, and in stumbled Linda Greenwood. She was bundled up in a tan puffy coat, a knit hat snugly pulled down over her ears, and a green scarf so voluminous it nearly concealed the lower half of her face. I only recognized it was Linda because of the distinctive coat she wore. She paused for a moment, swiftly pulled off her dark blue gloves, and stuffed them into the pockets of her coat, then unwrapped the scarf from around her face. Catching sight of us, her eyes widened and she quickly made her way over.

"Good morning, Allie, Lucy," she greeted, pulling out a chair from our table without waiting for an invitation and sitting down. "The weather is just dreadful outside. Don't even get me started on why I thought it was a good idea to venture out today," she said with a chuckle. "But it sure is cozy and warm in here."

I nodded in agreement. "It wasn't snowing when we left our homes, but it seems we'll be driving back in it."

"How have you been, Linda?" Lucy asked. "We haven't seen you in such a long time."

Linda's grin revealed rosy, pink cheeks, flushed from the bitter cold. "I'm doing wonderfully. Actually, I've been meaning to call you, Allie. It's fortunate I ran into you two," she said, turning to me. "Allie, I'm having a romantic weekend at my bed and breakfast the weekend before Valentine's Day, and I was wondering if you could prepare some Valentine-themed treats?"

Linda was the owner of the Bluebell Cottage B&B.

She was in her late fifties and occasionally requested my baking skills for special events. I brightened at the thought of making some romantic treats. "Of course, I can do that. What were you thinking of?"

Leaning back in her chair, her eyes sparkling with enthusiasm, she said, "I'm thinking chocolate-dipped strawberries, perhaps some raspberry tartlets, strawberry muffins, and maybe scones, too. I'm hosting a brunch the Saturday before Valentine's Day. There will be champagne, along with choices of blackberry pancakes and some egg dishes. I'd love to offer something sweet and charming to accompany the coffee and tea."

"I have some adorable, heart-shaped tartlet pans that would be perfect for Valentine's Day," I replied.

Linda nodded, her gaze momentarily drifting to the short queue at the counter before returning to me. "That sounds wonderful. Do you think you'll have any trouble sourcing strawberries at this time of year? Nice ones?"

"I'll check with Steve Anderson at the co-op. He's likely to have a source for them, and they'll surely be sweeter than the ones from the grocery store," I assured her.

"I hadn't thought to ask him," Linda admitted, glancing at Lucy. "The strawberries from the grocery store are so bland this time of year. I'm sure he'll find a source for some that are much tastier. Oh, I'm so glad we bumped into each other today. This has got me so excited for our Valentine's Day event. Lucy, I love your hair. Very appropriate for Valentine's Day."

"Thanks, Linda. Is the B&B fully booked for that weekend?" Lucy asked, pausing to take a sip of her coffee.

Linda nodded in confirmation. "Oh, yes, all the rooms were reserved before Christmas, except for one. But that final room was just booked a few days ago. It looks like I'll have a B&B full of Valentine's Day enthusiasts," she said, her expression turning to a frown. "Except for the last reservation. It's a gentleman who seems to be alone." She shrugged. "Well, I hope he doesn't mind being the only single person amidst happy, love-struck couples."

Lucy waved a dismissive hand. "He's probably some guy who hasn't got a romantic bone in his body and didn't even realize it was the weekend before Valentine's Day when he booked it. You know how clueless some men can be." She gave me a knowing look.

I returned the smile. "Some men just don't pick up on the hints. But having a full house is always great for your business, right, Linda?"

"Absolutely. I particularly adore Valentine's Day, so I'm very much looking forward to it. I've placed an order for lots of fresh flowers, and I'm planning to decorate."

Changing the subject, I asked, "How's Annie doing?" Annie was Linda's older sister who had recently moved in with her to help manage the B&B.

Linda rolled her eyes and leaned in closer across the table. "I'll tell you something, I love my sister, but she can be incredibly challenging. She agreed to help with the B&B, yet I struggle to get her to lift a finger. And when she does assist, it's rarely done correctly." She clucked and shook her head.

"That's unfortunate," I sympathized. "I thought she would be a big help to you."

Shaking her head again, Linda responded, "I thought so too. I know she felt isolated after her husband passed, but perhaps she was better off in Utah."

I was sorry to hear the sisters weren't getting along. Annie was a kind-hearted woman who, ten years ago, had married and moved away. It was only last year had lost her husband, leading her to return home to Sandy Harbor.

"Maybe she's still mourning her husband," Lucy suggested. "Dealing with the death of a spouse has to be incredibly difficult. If you give her some time, she might adjust."

I nodded in agreement. "Yes, the grief of losing a

spouse takes a long time to process." Having experienced it myself, I could empathize, and I hoped never to go through it again.

Linda glanced over her shoulder at the shortening line at the front counter and then turned back to us. "You're probably right. I should be more patient with her. Now, if you'll excuse me, I'm going to join that line and grab a hot, comforting drink," she said with a meaningful look, standing up. "Allie, you come up with some romantic, sweet treats for the brunch, and let me know. I'll have six couples and one single guest, and I'd like a nice variety for them all."

"I'll get on it and call you within a couple of days," I assured her. As she made her way to the counter, I turned to Lucy. "This is going to be fun."

She agreed, cradling her coffee cup with both hands. "Absolutely. I'm here to help with anything you need."

There's just something about Valentine's Day that I absolutely love, and I couldn't wait to start creating sweet treats for Linda's guests.

CHAPTER 2

I reviewed my list of the ingredients needed to prepare Valentine's treats for Linda's B&B while my granddaughter, Lilly, sat contently in her highchair. She babbled and cooed, amusing herself with a set of small, stackable cups. Her strawberry-blond hair was growing thicker by the day and her pink cheeks reminded me of my daughter Jennifer at that age. I might have been biased, but to me, Lilly was the most adorable baby I had ever laid eyes on.

"Lilly, what would you like for Valentine's Day? You know it's your birthday, too. It's your very first one, and we must celebrate it in style," I said with a smile. She might not have understood a word I said, but it didn't matter. She knew she was loved. Born on

Valentine's Day the previous year, her first birthday was an event I was excited about, especially since I was going to make her birthday cake. My daughter-in-law Sarah and I had been going over flavors and designs and had settled on strawberry for her smash cake and vanilla with strawberry cream filling for a larger cake for everyone else. My husband Alec had insisted on frosting bunnies, and Sarah wanted lilies in the design.

Returning to my list, I read over the items I had decided on: strawberries dipped in white, dark, and milk chocolate, some adorned with sprinkles and others with a delicate dusting of cocoa powder, raspberry tartlets with a drizzle of chocolate in all three varieties, strawberry scones, and a dark chocolate fudge cake. Linda would handle the brunch items, leaving me to focus on these delightful confections. Dave at the co-op had already assured me he'd supply the hothouse-grown strawberries and raspberries.

Lilly's squeal of delight drew my attention as she successfully stacked two cups. "Look at you! Such a clever girl," I exclaimed, watching her beam with pride over her achievement.

My black cat, Dixie, rose from his spot on the rug in front of the sink and walked over, sitting down before me with a plaintive "Meow."

I looked at him squarely. "It's not time to eat,

Dixie. If you're pestering me for canned food, you can return to your rug and nap," I told him firmly. Boundaries are sometimes necessary, even with those we adore. He responded by calmly grooming his paw, accepting the gentle rebuke.

After confirming the dessert plans with Linda, a grocery store visit was imminent.

The sound of the front door announced Alec's return. "Hello!" he called out cheerfully.

"Hello to you, too," I replied, grinning as he hurried over to Lilly's highchair. Her face lit up with joy at the sight of him. "How's my best girl?" he asked, planting a kiss on her head.

"Best girl? Isn't that title mine?" I teased.

Without missing a beat, he continued to dote on Lilly, chuckling as he tickled her chin before bestowing another kiss. "Oh, you are," he assured me. "Without you, I wouldn't have Lilly."

I let out a snort. "Thanks. At least I'm important, I guess." Setting my list and pen on the kitchen island, I made my way to the pantry to see what supplies I already had.

"Of course you are." He turned back to the baby. "Who is the prettiest girl?" He cooed in a high-pitched, playful voice. It was surprising to think that Alec, who I never expected to use baby talk or make silly faces at another female, was doing just that now.

A few years back, the idea would have seemed ridiculous. Yet, there he was, utterly smitten with our granddaughter. Lilly responded with some indistinct babble and extended a yellow stacking cup toward him.

"Thank you," he said warmly, accepting the cup from her. "This is the most beautiful cup I've ever seen."

I couldn't help but chuckle. "Be careful of spoiling her too much."

He glanced back at me with a smile. "Spoiling her is precisely my role. It's the whole reason she's here—for me to dote on her."

I continued smiling to myself as I rummaged through the pantry shelves and found some white dipping chocolate. Alec, who didn't have any biological children of his own, had embraced my son and daughter as his own, and by extension, my son's first child. He was a wonderful grandfather. There was no point in telling him not to spoil her. It was already done.

"How was work?" I asked, discovering a packet of pink-tinted white chocolate on the shelf. Pink dipped strawberries would be fun.

"You know how it is. Crime never takes a day off," he replied.

Turning back to him, I asked, "Oh? Anything interesting happen?"

He lifted Lilly out of her highchair and shook his head as he held her close. "Not really, unless you count a break-in at the feed store as interesting. Seems someone was desperate to get their hands on horse feed."

I let out a laugh and returned my attention to my list. "Well, who can blame them? It is horse feed, after all."

Alec walked over with Lilly in his arms and peered at the list of ingredients on the counter. "What's this for?"

I looked up at him. "Lucy and I had coffee at the Cup and Bean, and we ran into Linda. She's hosting a Valentine's Day brunch at the B&B and asked if I could prepare some special treats."

He nodded in understanding. "Sounds like a perfect match for you. Valentine's Day and chocolate."

I agreed with a nod. "It is. I've got all sorts of delightful ideas in mind, but I believe the pièce de résistance will be a selection of chocolate-dipped strawberries. Doesn't that sound tasty? I adore chocolate-dipped strawberries."

He leaned in and kissed me. "Chocolate-dipped strawberries do sound like fun. But what about us? What are our plans for Valentine's Day?"

I had thought that he would have made plans for Valentine's Day, as he had done every other year since we'd met. "You didn't make plans for Valentine's Day?" I asked, a hint of disappointment in my voice as I placed the pen back on the counter. "It's fine. I'll whip up something for dinner, and we'll have a romantic evening at home."

He flashed a grin. "You're so easily fooled. Of course, I made arrangements. We're having dinner at Antonio's in Portland."

My eyebrow arched in pleasant surprise. Antonio's was where he had taken me on our first Valentine's Day. I had embarrassed myself, thinking he was going to ask me to marry him then, but it still held fond memories for me. "Italian food? You know that's my favorite. I'll have the chance to dress up. It's been forever since I last wore a dress."

"I know it's your favorite, that's why I chose it. But what about this little lady? Valentine's Day is her birthday. How will we celebrate both?"

"Sarah wants to postpone the celebration until the following Saturday so she can invite Lilly's friends," I said.

His expression showed confusion. "Lilly has friends?"

"Absolutely," I assured him, affectionately

pinching Lilly's cheek. "My girl will be the star of any party she attends—just wait and see."

He chuckled. "You mean our girl. I had no idea she was already quite the socialite."

I smiled. "You're not paying close enough attention. This girl is destined for great things." Being a grandmother was the most wonderful thing that had ever happened to me. It seemed like just yesterday I was changing my own children's diapers. Yet, I found being a grandmother even more enjoyable than motherhood, mostly because the weighty responsibilities of raising children were no longer on my shoulders.

Lilly's babble interrupted my thoughts, and I looked at her, eyes wide with delight. "Did you hear that? She just said 'Mimi.'"

Alec gave Lilly a skeptical look and then disagreed. "No, she didn't say 'Mimi.' She said 'Granddad.'"

I narrowed my eyes at him playfully. "She didn't say anything that sounded even remotely like 'Granddad.' Her first word is going to be 'Mimi.'" Both Thad and Sarah claimed she had uttered 'Mama' and 'Dada,' but I had yet to hear those words from her. And 'Granddad' seemed quite unlikely. 'Mimi,' felt like a real possibility.

"She didn't say 'Mimi,'" he persisted.

"Oh, but she did. You need to be more observant. She definitely said 'Mimi.'" I reached out to take her from him, but to my amusement, she shook her head and clung to Alec.

He laughed triumphantly. "See? She said 'Granddad.' She adores her granddad and wants to stay with me."

I rolled my eyes, conceding, with a smile. "Yes, she loves her granddad—I won't dispute that—but she clearly said 'Mimi.'" With a chuckle, I turned back to the pantry to continue my search for ingredients.

He laughed harder. "She didn't say 'Mimi.' Don't fool yourself."

Shaking my head, I didn't bother to answer him. One thing was for certain: Lilly was profoundly attached to her granddad.

CHAPTER 3

"These strawberries smell amazing," Lucy said as she laid parchment paper on cookie sheets. "So sweet."

I nodded. "Don't they? Dave outdid himself with these."

"Where did he get them from? I can't imagine them growing here in Maine this time of year."

She had a point. The ground was still solidly frozen, and these strawberries hadn't grown in it. But they *were* from Maine. "They did grow in Maine. Near Bangor, there's a supplier who grows a lot of their produce in greenhouses. I'd love to have a greenhouse in my backyard."

"Would you? I guess it would be nice to have strawberries in your backyard in the middle of winter." She finished covering the pans with parchment paper and came to stand beside me as I melted white, dark, and milk chocolate in the microwave, being vigilant to keep it from scorching.

"I think it would be wonderful, but I don't know if I'd be willing to put in the work that would be required. Now then, I think we'll dip the strawberries in the chocolate and then coat some of them with sprinkles, nuts, and crushed candy. They shouldn't take too long to dry, then we can put them in the boxes to take to Linda's." I had already separated the prettiest strawberries to be dipped from the ones that weren't quite as nice. Those strawberries would go into making strawberry scones and would be just as delicious.

She nodded and picked up a large berry, dipping it into the glass bowl of melted milk chocolate. I placed the cookie sheets on the counter in front of us.

"These are going to be sensational," she said as she sprinkled pastel-colored sprinkles on the berry and laid it on the parchment paper.

"I think so too. I love Valentine's Day. It's the precursor to spring and gives me a little lift out of the winter doldrums." I picked up a large strawberry and quickly dipped it into white chocolate.

She nodded knowingly. "That stretch between Christmas and Valentine's Day is long. With all the snow and overcast skies, it can get a little depressing. But once Valentine's Day arrives, that's when I start thinking about spring and all the flowers and greenery outside."

I picked up two large strawberries, one in each hand, and dipped one in white chocolate and the other in dark chocolate. It didn't matter what kind of chocolate you preferred; it made the strawberries even tastier. Once thoroughly coated, I laid the white chocolate berry down on the parchment paper and gave it a quick sprinkle of pink and red chunky sugar, then dipped the dark chocolate berry into the white sprinkles. We tried to make them as fun and creative as we could, and I was sure that Linda would be pleased with them.

"Are you going to get the tarts and scones finished in time?" she asked, dipping a strawberry into white chocolate.

I nodded without looking up. "Yes, they won't take long. When we finish with the strawberries, we'll get to work on the tartlets. The scones won't take very long, and I predict we will be finished by late afternoon."

We finished with the strawberries, and I went to pour myself a cup of coffee and take a break. The kitchen was chilly, but it would warm up as soon as we got the tartlets in the oven.

"These turned out great," Lucy said, looking over the drying strawberries. "I could eat a dozen of them myself."

"You and me both," I said. "There are some extras, though, so help yourself." I had made sure to buy plenty of strawberries from Dave at the co-op so that we could test them out. I also planned on delivering some to my son, Thad and Sarah, as well as sending some home with Lucy.

Lucy joined me at the coffee pot, and I poured a cup for her.

"Thanks." She stirred creamer into her cup.

I sighed. "Did you remind Ed that it's Valentine's Day?" I knew it was pointless, but part of me clung to the hope that he would do something for her.

She rolled her eyes and nodded. "Oh, sure, I reminded him. He said that Valentine's Day was for kids."

I snorted. "I guess there's no hope for that one."

She took a sip of her coffee, cradling the cup between her hands. "Nope. And like I said before, I've given up on it. Is your mother coming to visit for Lilly's first birthday?"

I shook my head. "No, she wanted to make a trip out, but she's having trouble with her hip and decided that the plane ride would be too much for her. She's hoping to make it when the weather's a little warmer."

"Oh, that's terrible. I'm sorry she's not feeling well, and I know she's going to be so upset to miss Lilly's first birthday."

I nodded and took a sip of my coffee. My mother had been quite upset about not being able to make the trip, but the cold here in Maine wouldn't have been good for her joints. "I promised her I would video everything and we would do a live video call with her, too."

"Thank goodness for technology so she can see what's going on. I bought Lilly a couple of outfits for her birthday."

I smiled. "I'm sure she'll love them. I bought her a rocking horse and some shoes."

"A rocking horse? She'll love that."

I headed to the kitchen counter to get started on the strawberry and raspberry tartlets. "If you can help me by measuring out the sugar and raspberries, that would be great."

"You bet," she said as she got to work on the filling while I got to work on making the crust. The tartlets would be a fun addition. I was going to make two dozen of them for Linda and half a dozen for Thad and Sarah, and send half a dozen home with Lucy. Ed might not have been big on Valentine's Day, but I could give her some sweet treats to celebrate with.

The front door slammed, and we looked at each

other. It was too early for Alec to be home. In a moment, my daughter Jennifer stood in the doorway, her cheeks pink from the cold and her eyes bright with excitement. "Hey." She spotted the strawberries and hurried over. "Chocolate-covered strawberries! My favorite."

"Those are for Linda Greenwood. I wasn't expecting you to drop by today." I laid out the heart-shaped tartlet pans on the counter.

She nodded. "I only have one class on Friday mornings, and I thought I'd come home for the weekend. What are you two doing? Why are the strawberries for Linda?"

"She asked me to make chocolate-dipped strawberries, tartlets, and scones for this weekend. She's having a Valentine's Day brunch on Sunday, and the B&B is fully booked."

"Oh, they look so delicious," she said. "I don't suppose you could spare one? Or two?"

"They are delicious," Lucy said. "I've had three."

"I made extras; go ahead. So, what are you up to, Jennifer? Do you have any plans for Valentine's Day?" I eyed her. Ever since she had broken up with her boyfriend last year, she hadn't mentioned a new man in her life.

She looked up at me, her eyes sparkling with excitement as she picked up a strawberry dipped in milk chocolate and sprinkled with white chunky sugar. "I have a date."

Lucy and I gasped. "Oh, how exciting," Lucy exclaimed. "Who is he? Do we know him?"

She shook her head, a smile playing on her lips. "I don't think you know him. But he's in my sociology class, and we've been talking for a while. We're going out on our first date on Valentine's Day. I can hardly wait."

This explained the light in her eyes and her buoyant mood. "I am so happy to hear that. What's his name? What is he studying?"

"He's going to be a writer. Can you believe it? His name is Josh Landry, and he's tall, with dark brown eyes and dimples. Dimples!" she nearly swooned.

I sighed, feeling a warm rush of maternal pride. "Oh, I'm so glad you've found someone," I said. "He sounds dreamy."

Jennifer rolled her eyes and laughed. "Dreamy?"

"Dreamy," I affirmed with a smile.

"I'm happy for you, too, sweetie." Lucy gave her a one-armed side hug. "He sounds fantastic, and I can hardly wait to meet him. Will you be bringing him around soon?"

She shrugged nonchalantly. "We're just going on our first date, so I don't think I'll be bringing him around just yet. But he's very sweet, and he's an introvert like me. We both love to read, and we talk about books all the time." She sighed contentedly and picked up a white chocolate strawberry. "I can hardly wait for our date."

"I bet you'll have a lot of fun," I said as I measured butter into a mixing bowl, watching my daughter. Jennifer was my high-strung, excitable child, and to hear that she was happy made my heart swell with joy.

I gave Lucy a knowing look. My girl was happy.

CHAPTER 4

Sunday dawned clear and bright, with the snow melting since we hadn't received fresh snowfall for several days. Alec assisted me in loading the scones, tartlets, and chocolate-dipped strawberries into the trunk of my car. After sharing a kiss, he set off for an early morning run while I drove to Lucy's house to pick her up.

"It's chilly out," she said as I navigated through the Cup and Bean drive-through to get us a little pick-me-up. Linda would likely have a pot of coffee brewing at the bed and breakfast already, but I expected that with the brunch preparations, she and her sister would be preoccupied. I wanted to avoid being underfoot.

I nodded in agreement. "You can say that again. I

probably should have worn an extra layer." The tip of my nose was cold despite the car's heater. Some mornings are simply like that—the biting cold hangs around the entire day.

Once at the bed and breakfast, we each picked up a box of tartlets and hurried to the back door leading to the kitchen, trying to keep the slipping and sliding to a minimum on the icy ground. I knocked, but there was no response. After waiting several minutes, I knocked with more force. Casting a glance at Lucy when there was still no answer, I raised my hand to knock again when we finally heard movement inside. Annie opened the back door, blinking at us through her thick-lensed glasses. Her expression was one of confusion. I wondered if Linda had informed her of our early morning delivery.

"Good morning, Annie," I greeted her cheerfully. "How are you today? We've brought the scones, tartlets, and chocolate-dipped strawberries for the brunch."

Understanding dawned in her eyes, and her face broke into a smile. "Good morning, ladies. Linda mentioned you'd be stopping by. It had just about slipped my mind," she admitted, stepping aside to allow us entry. "We've been working like mad to get things prepared for the big day."

We scurried past her into the cozy warmth of the kitchen, where Linda was preparing what appeared to be pancakes. She greeted us with a smile. "Good morning, ladies. I'm so relieved you arrived early. A couple of my guests mentioned they wanted their breakfast earlier than I had scheduled, so it's fortuitous that you're here." She smiled, but she looked harried.

We placed the boxes on the kitchen island. "I thought it best that we arrive bright and early, just in case of such an occurrence," I said. "It smells good in here."

Linda's smile widened. "I'm making blackberry pancakes for the brunch. They're my favorite."

"That sounds tasty," Lucy said. "I should have reserved a room for myself, considering the wonderful brunch you're hosting."

Linda chuckled. "You mean just for yourself, not for you and your husband?"

Lucy shook her head. "No, just for me. My husband is indifferent to Valentine's Day, but I would adore some of those pancakes."

Linda laughed again. "Oh, Lucy, you're such a card. One of these days, I'll invite you both for a midweek breakfast. I seldom have guests then, and we could savor a delightful meal by the fireplace without interruption."

"That sounds marvelous," Lucy responded with enthusiasm. "Count me in."

"Me too," I added. "We're going to get the rest of the goodies from my trunk, and we'll be right back."

Braving the cold again, we retrieved the clear plastic boxes holding the strawberries and the bakery box of scones. "They look exquisite, don't they?" Lucy remarked, admiring our handiwork.

I nodded in agreement. "They're absolutely tempting." Making the strawberries was as much fun as eating them, and I planned on making a small batch for Alec and me later.

We hastened back inside and placed the strawberries and scones alongside the other baked goods. Linda had already lifted the lids off the tartlet boxes, and she turned to me with a wide grin. "I knew you would do a splendid job. These both look and smell delectable. And the strawberries—they're so large and pretty, and you've decorated them beautifully."

I couldn't help but smile. Compliments from my customers were my greatest reward. "Thank you. We sampled some scones and tartlets, and I must say, they turned out exceptionally well—not to toot my own horn."

"The raspberry tartlets are my favorite," Lucy said. "I assisted Allie with the mixing, but the credit goes to her."

"They do look scrumptious," Annie remarked in a hopeful tone. "Perhaps there will be a couple left over for me to try."

"Annie, could you please set the tables?" Linda directed, her voice carrying a slight sharpness. I noticed the edge, but Annie seemed unbothered and proceeded to the dining room without comment. Linda then looked at us with a knowing expression. "Honestly, I must instruct her on every little task. She never takes the initiative."

I wasn't sure how to respond to Linda's frankness, so I offered a sympathetic smile instead. "With so much to manage here, I imagine it's challenging to know where to start."

Linda emitted a soft noise of exasperation and returned her attention to the pancakes. "The work never seems to end, but I genuinely enjoy what I do. It's a joy to meet such a variety of interesting people and to share stories about our quaint town."

"It certainly sounds enjoyable," Lucy agreed, shooting me a look.

We visited for a few minutes, and as we were getting ready to leave, a scream from another room pierced the calm. The three of us exchanged wide-eyed looks.

"That's Annie. She's likely seen what she believes to be a spider. I can't fathom why she doesn't exercise better judgment than to scream like that. She'll scare the guests," Linda huffed. She sighed in frustration, and turned toward the kitchen doorway when Annie shrieked again.

"That doesn't sound like she's seen a spider," I said. Lucy and I hurried through the doorway and into the parlor. The bed and breakfast was adorned in shabby chic decor, featuring an old-fashioned sitting room next to the kitchen.

"The scream came from upstairs," Lucy pointed out. I nodded, and we ascended the stairs, where we were met by a flustered couple emerging from a bedroom at the top of the staircase. The woman was clad in a red and pink fuzzy bathrobe, while the man was dressed in a T-shirt and pajama pants. They stopped; their faces etched with concern.

"What's happening?" the woman asked.

I shook my head, showing our shared confusion, as Lucy and I continued up the steps. "I'm not certain," I replied.

We reached the top of the stairs quickly, where Annie appeared from one of the adjacent bedrooms. Her face was ashen, and she was visibly distressed. "Call the police," she instructed tersely.

"What?" I asked, bewildered. "What's happened?"

Annie merely shook her head, her expression

grave. "Something dreadful has occurred to Mr. Taylor. We need the police immediately."

I paused, glancing back at the couple who had just joined us from another room. "What's the issue?" the man asked.

Before she could answer, I moved past Annie and into the bedroom, where a man lay motionless on the floor, his eyes fixed on the ceiling. He was dressed in jeans and a light blue sweatshirt, and it was stained with blood. One shoe was on his foot while the other was placed in front of the side of the bed, as if he had been preparing to be getting ready for bed after venturing outside or he had gotten up early to go somewhere and was disturbed before he could finish dressing.

I rushed to his side and knelt, searching for a pulse while turning away from the grim sight of the blood-soaked sweatshirt. Lucy arrived behind me and inhaled sharply upon seeing the scene. She withdrew her phone from her pocket. "Is he alive?" she whispered urgently.

I shook my head after failing to find a pulse. "No, he's gone." I didn't recognize the man. "I'll call Alec." I retrieved my phone from my coat pocket and called Alec.

"Hello?" Alec answered, breathing hard as he ran.

"Alec, we need you at the Bluebell Bed and Breakfast. There's been a homicide," I whispered into the phone.

I could hear Alec's heavy breaths as he halted his run. After a brief pause, he responded, "A homicide at the B&B? Did I hear you right?"

"Yes, I haven't called anyone else yet," I said.

"I'm nearby. I'll take care of reporting it," he said. "Try to keep people away from the crime scene. I'll be right there."

After hanging up the phone and placing it back into my pocket, I turned to find Annie, Linda, and several guests clustered in the doorway, their gazes fixed on the lifeless figure. Linda's voice carried a note of trepidation. "Oh, no," she murmured. "Please don't say it."

I simply shook my head; words were unnecessary.

"What was his name?" another woman asked, her tone somber.

"That's Mr. Taylor," Linda identified him. "He was the gentleman who arrived alone." Her eyes met mine.

I sighed. "The police have been called and will arrive shortly. We had all better step outside and close the door to preserve the scene."

There was a moment of hesitation before everyone withdrew, allowing Lucy and me to exit the room. I carefully shut the door behind us.

Linda moaned, "Why must this occur under my roof?" She surveyed her guests, who had emerged from their rooms, with a look of apology. "I am tremendously sorry, ladies and gentlemen. However, I must return to preparing brunch, which will be served in no more than thirty minutes."

The guests seemed less than enthusiastic about the prospect of a meal, and understandably so. Linda hastened down the stairs to the kitchen, calling over her shoulder, "Annie, your help is required!"

Exchanging glances, Lucy and I both knew that breakfast was the least of our concerns at the moment. But maybe it would distract the guests.

CHAPTER 5

While the police worked on Mr. Taylor upstairs, Lucy and I helped Linda and Annie whip up the brunch she had planned on serving later in the morning. I wasn't sure anyone would be in the mood to eat, but it was better than standing around thinking about what had happened.

"I just can't believe something like this happened," Annie said as she waited for Linda to finish filling a platter with blackberry pancakes. Annie seemed in shock as she went about her duties getting the brunch ready.

"My goodness, these pancakes smell good, if I do say so myself," Linda said as she flipped one over. "I love fruit with my breakfast, or rather brunch. I think these are the perfect pancakes to serve for a Valentine's Day brunch, don't you?" she said to no one in particular. "There's lox and bagels in the fridge and, of course, champagne. What's a Valentine's Day brunch without champagne? And I made an egg casserole—it's warming in the oven."

"The pancakes smell wonderful," Lucy said, glancing at me. "I love fruit with my breakfast, too." Lucy shot me another look. The sisters seemed to have different ways of dealing with the tragedy that had just occurred in the B&B. Annie was spacey and having trouble accepting it while Linda pretended nothing had gone awry with her Valentine's Day brunch plans.

"Allie, did Alec say what he thought happened?" Annie asked, still dutifully holding the platter.

I shook my head. "I haven't had a moment to speak to him since he arrived. I probably won't until later tonight when he comes home." There were a handful of police officers on the scene now, combing through the upstairs rooms. Linda's guests were sent to wait in the dining room. Every time I walked into the room with either the coffee, the silverware, or anything I was putting on the table, they all anxiously asked me what was going on and if I knew anything. One couple, Andrea and Tom Thompson, were local, but the other couples were from out of town, so they didn't know that I was married to the lead detective on the case unless Andrea or Tom told them. But I told them exactly what I knew, which was nothing. It would take a while for the police to process the crime scene.

Annie nodded. "Of course not."

Linda stood back from the kitchen island and looked over the food she had prepared. "There now. I think we're ready to serve our guests. Would you ladies help me take the food to the dining room?"

I nodded. "Of course." I picked up a platter of scrambled eggs, and Lucy picked up the scones, and we headed to the dining room.

"So, is there anything new?" A young woman asked anxiously as we entered the dining room. If I remember right, Linda said her name was Alana Davidson. She was here with her fiancé, Ken Rhodes.

I shook my head. "No, it's going to take a while for the police to process the scene," I reminded her for what felt like the hundredth time. "In the meantime, Linda has made this delicious breakfast for you all." We set the food on a table draped in a white tablecloth with red hearts at the head of the room. The guests could pick out what they wanted buffet style.

"Yes, yes, why don't you all just dig in? We have a few more dishes to bring out but don't hesitate to help yourselves to the food. And if anybody needs more coffee, there's plenty of it here in the coffee pot," Linda tapped the top of the large silver coffee pot at the end of the table with her fingers.

"I just don't understand it," Andrea said as she got to her feet. She glanced at her husband beside her. "Who on earth would kill that man? And how come nobody heard a thing?"

"You never know what people have gotten themselves into," an elderly man, Joe Donaldson, said from the other end of the room. "People do such stupid things sometimes. Get involved with people who are up to no good." He shook his head in disgust.

His wife, Brenda, stood up. She was wearing a blue bathrobe, and her hair was in curlers. Once the police had arrived, no one was allowed back into their rooms.

"He seemed like a nice man," Brenda said. "I ran into him in the hallway yesterday morning, and although he didn't have much to say, he was polite. He said 'excuse me' when he accidentally stepped into my path. You can tell a lot about people by how polite they are. I am certain that he had nothing to do with his own death."

"He wasn't nice," Amanda Rupert spoke up. "Every time I ran into him in this place, he was rude. Snooty. He looked down his nose at me like there was something wrong with me." She sat up in her seat, clearly offended by her encounters with the deceased. Her husband, Dale, got up to look over the food on the table without commenting.

Alana nodded. "Exactly. When I was heading out the front door at the same time he was, he all but shoved me out of his way. Didn't say 'excuse me' or anything. I've never dealt with anybody so rude."

There were nods around the room.

"Did anybody have any long conversations with him?" I asked. Lucy and I made eye contact for a moment. We were gathering intel on our next case. When you're married to a detective, you take an interest in these types of things.

They all shook their heads. "No, he wasn't the talkative sort. I tried to talk to him about the weather, and I asked if he was meeting his Valentine here at the B&B, but he just snorted, shook his head, and walked away. Didn't even bother answering me," Andrea said.

"He didn't sound friendly," Lucy said, turning to me.

I nodded. "But he was new to Sandy Harbor, wasn't he? Had he been here before?" I glanced at Linda.

Linda set the chocolate-covered strawberries down on the table. "I've just got to get a few condiments from the refrigerator. I'll be right back."

"Linda," I said before she could leave the room.

"Had Mr. Taylor stayed here at the B&B before? Or have you seen him around town?"

She hesitated and shook her head. "No, he's never stayed here before. Why?"

I shrugged. "We were all just wondering about him, is all."

She shook her head, smiling. "I'm sure the police will sort things out. Let me go get those condiments. Annie, come help."

Annie followed her younger sister dutifully out of the room, and Lucy and I gazed at one another. Something was going on here, but I wasn't quite sure what it was. Or maybe it was just that Linda seemed so distracted. I suppose if somebody was murdered in my B&B, I might be distracted too, but I wasn't sure.

Lucy sidled up to me. "What do you think?"

I shook my head. "I don't know yet. It's too soon to know what's really going on."

"That Mr. Taylor was on his telephone all the time," Annie suddenly said from behind me.

I jumped and whirled around, surprised she was standing there when I thought she had left the room. "Was he?"

She nodded. "Every time I saw him, he was on his phone. Even though it was cold outside, he was frequently out on the back patio. He complained that we didn't have a fire pit out there for him. Linda said she was going to make some sort of fire pit for him, but we didn't have anything to make one with."

"But he still went out there in the cold?" I asked.

She nodded. "I thought that was strange. Why didn't he just take his phone calls inside? He had a fireplace in his room."

That was true. I had seen it when I had gone in to check on Annie's screaming. "Did you overhear any of his conversations?"

She shook her head. "No, not one. Every time he noticed me, he would get really quiet, and he would turn his back to me and speak in a whisper into the phone."

"Annie!" Linda called from the kitchen.

Annie rolled her eyes. "I can't have a moment's peace around here. If you'll excuse me."

I nodded as she turned and headed back to the kitchen. I looked at Lucy. "Lots of secretive phone calls."

She stepped closer to me. "I wonder if he was paranoid that the walls were thin and somebody might overhear his conversation, and that's why he went out onto the patio?"

I nodded. "Or maybe he thought there was some sort of electronic device in the room that might record his conversation." Maybe our victim was the paranoid type? This was all very interesting, and I wondered what Alec was discovering upstairs.

"This isn't my idea of a romantic Valentine's Day getaway," Alana grumbled.

Amanda shook her head. "Mine either. I swear, after all of this, we're going to have to go away for another weekend trip." She looked at her husband pointedly. He stood up and headed over to the buffet table, ignoring her. She rolled her eyes, got up, and followed him.

I didn't know what had happened to Mr. Taylor, but if he didn't know anybody in town, then it was likely that somebody in this room had murdered him. But why?

CHAPTER 6

I heard Alec's key turn in the lock, and I jumped up from where I had been impatiently waiting on the couch and hurried to the front door. When it swung open, I grinned. "Hey, stranger! It's been a while."

He smiled and nodded, wrapping me in his arms. "It's been a long while." He kissed the side of my neck, and we stood there for a few moments. He was still dressed in his running clothes from this morning, and I knew he must be exhausted. He finally released his grip on me and stepped back. "I am beat."

I nodded. "I bet you are. I made meatloaf for dinner. I'll warm you up a plate."

He sighed and followed me into the kitchen. "It's

really unnecessary. Yancey picked up dinner for us earlier."

I ignored him and went to the refrigerator, removed the meatloaf and mashed potatoes, and set them on the counter. "How long ago was that, though? I bet it was a long time ago." I knew once he and his team got to work on a case that meals were a second thought.

He got a bottle of water from the refrigerator. "You're right, I think it was around six."

"And it's 11:42 now. So, I'm going to heat a plate up for you, and when you're done eating, we'll get you to bed."

He nodded and sat down at the kitchen table. "I tell you, I don't know if I'll ever get used to the long hours that are necessary on the first days of a murder case. You would think that I would."

I shook my head as I put the food on a plate, then stuck it in the microwave. "I'm sure there's so much that must go into a new investigation. Plus, there are all the emotions of the people you're talking to, and that has got to take a toll on you, making you even more tired than you would be if it was just an ordinary job with long hours."

He nodded. "You're right. The worst part of my job is telling someone their loved one has been murdered."

I turned back to him. "Did you find out anything?"

He sat back in his chair. "I didn't find any evidence that points to anybody there at the B&B being the murderer. And he was in town to settle his great aunt's estate."

I frowned. "Why would he stay at a romantic B&B to settle his great aunt's estate? Everyone else was celebrating Valentine's Day a few days early."

He nodded. "I called his wife, and she said he wasn't the romantic type, and he didn't care about it being Valentine's Day weekend. She said none of the other motels in town had vacancies."

The bell on the microwave dinged, and I brought the plate and some silverware to the table. "Here you go. Nice and hot. But it's weird that all the other motels in town were booked. I mean, we're a scenic beach town, and I can see where some people would want to come here to get away, but our weather isn't the greatest in February, and they're not going to the beach in this cold."

He nodded as he cut into his meatloaf with the side of his fork. "That's true. I mean, I can see people wanting to get away to a sweet little B&B like Linda's; it is pretty nice there. I hadn't been there before. But you're right, who would want to stay at a regular old motel in a beach town where you can't go to the beach? I suppose they could go to the beach, but they'd freeze their tails off." He took a bite of his meatloaf and nodded. "Excellent, as usual."

I smiled. "Thank you. Didn't his wife think it was weird that he was staying at a B&B? Linda said he was the only singleton there for the weekend, and she acted like she didn't know why that was. When you talked to her, did she mention if she knew he was there to handle his great aunt's estate?"

He shook his head. "No, she said he kept to himself, and he was gone a lot."

"Annie said he was on his phone a lot and would go outside, even though it was cold. I suppose he had business to deal with for the estate. Lawyers and such, but would they really be working on the weekend?" My mind was already churning with questions. There had to be a reason he was murdered the way he was, and I was going to get to the bottom of it. My black cat, Dixie, sauntered into the kitchen, then stopped, looking at the two of us, and blinked as if he didn't understand what we were doing in the kitchen at this time of night.

"Dixie, have we invaded your space?" He ignored me and went to his food bowl and started crunching on his food. I turned back to Alec. "What about the other guests? Could he have had a problem with one of them?"

He took a sip of his water. "They seemed confused

and horrified that someone was murdered in the same B&B they were staying at."

I watched him eat for a few minutes. Then I asked, "What about his wife? How did she react when you talked to her?"

He was quiet for a moment, and then he turned back to his plate of food and took a bite of mashed potatoes. When he swallowed, he looked at me again. "It seemed odd. She didn't seem as surprised as I would have imagined she would be to find out her husband was killed while away on business."

"Really? Her husband was away on business, staying in a romantic B&B, and was murdered, and yet his wife isn't that surprised. I have to come back to the question: who stays in a romantic B&B if they're on a business trip? He could have stayed at a regular motel in Bangor." None of this added up.

He nodded. "I have that same question. She's coming to town on Tuesday, and I will talk to her more in-depth then."

"Did she know who might have wanted to kill him?"

He shook his head. "No. She couldn't understand why he had been murdered or who might have done it, but at the same time, there wasn't much reaction or emotion about it."

"Where is he from? Does he have kids?"

"He's from New Hampshire. They used to live here, but they moved away ten years ago. She said that when they sold his aunt's house, they would say goodbye to Sandy Harbor for good."

"Well, that sounds like she didn't exactly like this town." I got up, poured myself a glass of milk, and brought the cookie jar to the table. I didn't need cookies this late at night, but that didn't mean I wasn't going to have some.

He shrugged. "She didn't say whether she disliked the town. I get the feeling she's a person who is all business. Or maybe she was just in shock."

I nodded and took the lid off the cookie jar, peering inside. It had been ages since I had baked any cookies, but I had picked some up from the bakery a few days earlier and put them inside. I fished out an oatmeal raisin cookie. "They both sound like they're a lot of fun." I looked at him with one eyebrow raised. There was something fishy about these people, but I couldn't quite put my finger on it. Not yet anyway.

He smiled tiredly. "Agreed. Something is going on there, and I am going to get to the bottom of it."

I took a bite of the cookie and smiled. It was perfectly soft and delicious. "Who was his great aunt?"

"Daisy Taylor."

I gasped. "Oh, no. I know Daisy. Oh, I guess I mean I knew her. She was a very sweet woman. I'm sorry to hear that she died."

"His wife said that she was 102."

I gasped again. "Really? I wouldn't have thought she was that old. I thought maybe late eighties at the most. She was always happy and chipper, and she liked to talk. I don't think I ever saw her have a blue day. That's a shame that she passed away. I guess I haven't been keeping up with the newspaper to see who died."

He chuckled. "That's the only reason you get that newspaper, isn't it?"

I nodded. "Yes. There comes a time in a person's life when their age makes them watch the obituaries."

He almost choked on his water. "Are you kidding me? You're not old enough to be worried about keeping an eye on the obituaries."

I was approaching an age that made me think about the obituaries more than I ever had. Maybe it was because I had become a grandmother in the past year, or maybe it was just the fact that fifty was right around the corner. But fifty was the new thirty, wasn't it? At least that's what I was telling myself.

"I just want to see if any of my friends have passed away. That's all."

He shook his head. "You are something else."

He finished his dinner, and we went up to bed, but it was more than an hour before I finally fell asleep. I felt bad that Daisy had passed away, and I wasn't even aware of it. I also wondered what had happened to Paul Taylor.

CHAPTER 7

Alec was up and out of the house earlier than I expected. I knew he had gotten very little sleep, and I felt bad for him. After I got a run in on my treadmill, Lucy and I agreed to meet at the Cup and Bean Coffee Shop. Just because we weren't running outside together didn't mean that we couldn't go for coffee afterward.

"I got the raspberry mocha again," Lucy said as she took a sip from her cup. "So good."

I nodded. "I got one too, and a raspberry muffin."

"I should've gotten one of those," she said regretfully. We turned around and spotted our friend, Mr. Winters, sitting at the corner table. He was glancing beneath it, and I knew that his little dog Sadie was there at his feet, lapping up the attention as she ate the whipped cream from a pup cup.

We headed over. "Good morning, Mr. Winters," I said.

He looked up from beneath the table and grinned. "Well, how are the two of you today? Cold enough for you?"

We sat down across from him, and I nodded. "It's definitely cold enough for us, and we're doing great. We were here the other day, but we didn't see you. I was worried you weren't feeling well."

His eyes widened. "Really? How come you didn't stop by to check on me then?"

Oh, he had me there. I shook my head. "It was only one day; it wasn't enough to call around to the hospitals to see if something had happened to you."

Lucy chuckled. "If you hadn't shown up today, we would have dropped by your house, I promise." Mr. Winters was elderly, and it wouldn't have hurt to check on him. Next time.

He nodded. "Well, I certainly would hope so." He smiled. "So, what's going on with the two of you? Anything new? Did I miss anything?"

This was a surprise. Mr. Winters usually heard all the news and gossip almost the moment something happened. Hadn't he heard that someone had been murdered at Linda Greenwood's B&B?

"There was a murder at the B&B," I hissed.

His eyes widened. "Really? When? Why don't I know about this?"

I shrugged. "I don't know. It sounds like you might be off your game. Are you sure you weren't ill?"

He narrowed his eyes at me. "I'm perfectly fine. When did it happen?"

"Yesterday," Lucy supplied. "Linda planned a Valentine's Day brunch for yesterday, and the body was discovered then. By us. Well, technically Linda's sister Annie found him, but we were Johnny on the spot when she screamed."

His brow furrowed. "Valentine's Day? Why was she having a Valentine's Day brunch yesterday when Valentine's Day isn't until the 14th, and that is on a Wednesday?"

I shook my head. "Most people don't take time off in the middle of the week to go to a B&B, so she had it the weekend before."

He nodded. "I see. How did he die? Who is he? Do we know him? How did you manage to be there when he was found?" Mr. Winters was trying to make up for lost time since he hadn't already heard about this.

"He's from out of town, and he was stabbed. That's all we know for now. Alec is on the case, of course, but he hasn't found out much yet," I said and took a sip of my coffee.

"Linda asked Allie to make some sweets for the brunch," Lucy informed him. "That's why we were there."

He nodded and pushed his glasses up on his nose. He had removed his coat, but he was wearing a red scarf around his neck, and a red knit hat covered his white hair. "Okay then, we've got to get looking. His name?"

"Paul Taylor," Lucy whispered.

He nodded. "I'll look into this. Don't you ladies worry, I'll find something out. Someone I know has to know something."

I leaned forward, glanced over my shoulder, and then back. "Did you know Daisy Taylor?"

His eyes widened, and he nodded. "Sure, I knew Daisy. Who didn't? Why?"

"I guess she passed away recently, and Paul was her great-nephew. He and his wife used to live here, and he was here to sort out the estate." I took a sip of my coffee.

He nodded again. "I heard Daisy passed away. The old gal was 102, from what I heard. She lived a good, long life, and she certainly was happy about it, too."

Lucy nodded. "I know. She was so sweet."

Mr. Winters was quiet for a few moments. Then he looked at me. "I know Linda Greenwood, too. I heard her sister moved back to town last year."

I nodded. "Yes, Annie moved in with her at the B&B to help her out. The poor thing lost her husband early last year."

He took a sip of his black coffee before saying anything more. "I always thought Linda was a bit jealous of Annie."

I hadn't heard this before. "Oh? Why do you say that?"

He shrugged. "Linda never married and doesn't have any children. Annie has three kids from her first marriage, and then she married that other fella when the first one died. There's just something about their relationship that I always thought was a bit off. The only thing I could come up with was that Linda was jealous of her sister."

Lucy and I looked at one another, and then I turned back to him. "I didn't know that."

He nodded. "I'm sure it doesn't have any relevance to the murder, but it was just something that came to mind now that you've brought up her B&B."

We looked up as the front door opened, and Linda, wearing her tan puffy coat, stumbled in, almost slipping and falling on the slick floor. Her eyes widened at her near accident, and then she turned in our direction. I gave her a little wave, and she smiled, looking embarrassed. She waved back and went to the front counter to get some coffee.

"Maybe we'll find out something new," Lucy whispered.

I nodded. "I hope so." I reached beneath the table and patted the little gray poodle who was waiting patiently there. A few moments later, Linda approached our table.

"How are you doing, Linda?" I asked. "It was a terrible what happened yesterday, wasn't it?"

She nodded. "You better believe it." She sat in the chair next to Mr. Winters without asking. "Hello, Mr. Winters. I can't get over it. Why on earth would somebody kill that man in my B&B? I mean, of all places. Why?"

Mr. Winters shook his head. "It's terrible, is what it is."

She sighed and took a sip of her coffee. "I talked to Alec for a long time yesterday. I certainly hope that he finds that man's killer. I'd hate for this case to go unsolved."

"I'm sure it won't go unsolved. You know how Alec is. He won't sleep until he catches the killer." It had been twenty-four hours. Why bring up anything about it going unsolved?

She nodded. "He's the best detective this town has ever had. I am so glad that we have him. I'm sure the killer won't be as happy about it."

"Oh, you better believe it," Lucy said. "The killer is

going to be very unhappy that Alec is on the case."

They would also be unhappy that Lucy, I, and Mr. Winters would also be on the case, although unofficially. We had the uncanny ability to find out things that helped with the case. Call it a sixth sense. Or maybe we were just nosy. I don't know.

"You know, that Paul Taylor was a difficult customer from the moment he stepped foot on my property," Linda said, looking around at all of us before continuing. "He did nothing but complain. First, he said there were too many flowers in the house, and I thought, too many flowers? It's Valentine's Day weekend! But he didn't seem to like them. Said he had allergies." She rolled her eyes. "Some people will complain about anything."

I nodded and took a sip of my coffee. "I love flowers. But I guess I can see where if somebody has allergies, it would be uncomfortable to have so many of them around. But you're right. It was Valentine's Day."

She nodded. "He arrived Saturday afternoon and demanded that we make an early meal for him. I wasn't going to do it because meals are served at six o'clock. But then Annie steps in and she assures him we will make him a special dinner." She rolled her eyes again. "That sister of mine doesn't think. We're not a restaurant. We don't have the manpower to be making meals at all different times of the day. When people make their reservations, I inform them of mealtimes, and they can either eat what I make when I make it, or they can go out to a restaurant. It doesn't make any difference to me."

"I would think it would be very difficult catering to everybody's needs if you didn't set some rules," Lucy agreed.

She nodded. "He demanded that because meals were included in the room's price, we should deliver it on demand. I was about to give him a piece of my mind before Annie stepped in." She made a face again. "I won't be catering to anyone like that again. I've had a long talk with my sister, so she knows that we just don't do things like that. Anyway, next, he didn't like the towels. They were too thin. He wanted thicker ones. Believe me, my towels are thick enough. Then he didn't like that the room was on the east side of the house. He didn't want the rising sun to be shining through his window. I told him that was the only room we had, and there wasn't anything I could do about it."

"What did he say to that?" I asked.

She shook her head. "He said he guessed it would have to do." She gulped her coffee and stood up. "Well, I've got to get running. I've got lots of errands to do this morning."

"It was good seeing you, Linda," I said. "And it sure was a shame that your brunch was ruined."

She sniffed and put her gloves back on. "It was, wasn't it? I had everything planned down to the last detail, and that man had to ruin it." She shook her head, picked up her cup, and said, "I'll talk to you all later." She turned and was out the door in a moment.

Lucy leaned forward. "She does seem to be a bit resentful of her sister."

"I told you," Mr. Winters said.

I nodded. "Seems like it."

She also didn't seem to be nearly as upset about a murder having happened at her B&B as I would have been. Never mind that her brunch had been ruined. But people handle things differently, so what are you going to do? Other than continue snooping for clues, I mean.

CHAPTER 8

The following day, Lucy and I stopped by the shoe store downtown to see if Andrea Thompson was working today. Andrea and Tom were the only local couple at the B&B on Sunday. I wanted to get her take on what had happened and see if she remembered anything new now that she'd had some time to think about things.

"Oh, look at those," Lucy said, running a finger along a pair of suede pumps sitting on a display just inside the shoe store. They were cinnamon brown and pretty as could be.

"I love those, but I don't seem to have very many places I can wear nice pumps to anymore. And besides, you know I'm all about comfort these days." My days of wearing tall spiky heels were long gone.

She nodded. "Yes, but the heel isn't that high. Two inches max, I think. I wish I had someplace to go so I had a reason to buy them."

"Alec and I are going out to Antonio's for dinner for Valentine's Day. Maybe you should come with us? I bet if we call down to the restaurant, we could make arrangements for two more people at our table."

She snorted, shaking her head. "No, it's Valentine's Day and the two of you need a nice, romantic dinner alone. You don't need Ed and me tagging along. Besides, I already bought myself some flowers and candy and used Ed's credit card. And you know what? I think I deserve a new pair of shoes." She looked at me with one eyebrow raised.

I nodded. "I think you do too, and I'm sure Ed would love for you to have some. He wouldn't want to deprive his wife."

She chuckled as Andrea approached us. "Well, hello, Allie, Lucy. How are you ladies this afternoon?"

I smiled at her. "We're great, Andrea. Things got kind of crazy on Sunday, didn't they?"

She stepped closer, nodding, her eyes going wide. "I never in a million years would have thought something like that would happen anywhere near me. I live such a boring, quiet life. Staying at the B&B and getting away from the kids was the most exciting thing I've done in twenty years." She laughed. "But it was kind of nice for a little excitement. Oh, that sounds terrible, doesn't it? I don't mean it was nice that somebody got murdered."

I shook my head. "I know what you mean, and it was shocking, to say the least."

"Are you ladies looking for some shoes?" she asked. She rolled her eyes. "Duh. You're in a shoe store."

Lucy picked up the pump from the display. "Have you got these in a size nine and a half?"

She nodded. "I think I do. I'll be right back." She hurried off to the back room, and Lucy set the pump back down on the display.

"Ed will have a fit, but I don't care. He should have made some sort of arrangements for Valentine's Day, and he probably would have ended up spending less money." We both laughed. Poor Ed. He was a good guy but often didn't think ahead.

Andrea returned shortly with a box of shoes. "You're in luck. I've got them in a nine and a half."

We moved over to the chairs and sat down, and Lucy removed her boot.

"Let me get a couple of nylons for you to try them on with," Andrea said, popping back behind the counter and grabbing a pair. We were the only customers in the store now, and I was glad of that. We could speak openly. She returned to us and handed the nylons to Lucy.

"Thanks, Andrea," Lucy said as she took her socks off. "I haven't bought a pair of pumps for myself in ages."

"A woman needs a new pair of pumps now and then," she said.

I looked up at her. "Andrea, what was your take on what happened at the B&B on Sunday? Did you notice anything unusual before Paul Taylor's body was found?"

She crossed her arms in front of herself and shook her head. "Not really. Like Annie said—he was on his phone a lot and kept to himself. He wasn't the friendliest sort of person, but he wasn't mean or hateful to anyone. He just appeared to me to be somebody who had a lot on his mind and maybe was kind of introverted. He didn't mix with people."

I nodded. "He didn't have any visitors at the B&B, did he?" I doubted anybody would stop by to visit him there, but if he was at a hotel, he might have, so why not at the B&B?

She shook her head. "If he did, I didn't see them. Has Alec said anything about the murder? Does he have any ideas about who did it?"

I shook my head. "You know how it goes. He'll be working on this for a bit, but he'll get it sorted out."

"You know, I've known Linda for a number of years, probably more than ten, and she's a very nice woman who runs a very nice B&B. I just love going there. My husband and I use it as a sort of mini-getaway from the kids now and then. But it seemed to me that Linda was nervous when we first checked in."

I gazed at her. "Nervous? What do you mean?"

She hesitated. "Well, when we checked in, and she was handing us the key to the room, she was just very talkative and seemed to be a bit distracted. I don't know, it probably has nothing to do with anything, but it was something that I noticed. She didn't seem quite like herself."

"Really?" Lucy said, as she slipped on the pumps and stood up. "Whoa." She wobbled a bit, but then took a step and smiled. "Say, these are comfy."

Andrea nodded. "I tried on a pair of them when they first came in, and I thought they were really nice. I would love to buy a pair, but I have more than enough pumps. And plus, with them being suede, I'd have to be careful about them not getting wet."

I nodded. "With the snow we've been getting, it would be tricky to wear them and keep them nice."

"We do have some waterproofing that we can put on them, though, if you do decide to buy them, Lucy," she said.

Lucy walked around the shop. "That's a good idea. I think I'm going to take them."

"That's great," she said. "I'll take them to the back and treat them for you."

"Andrea, did you notice anything unusual about Annie? I mean, how was her relationship with Linda?" This probably had nothing to do with the murder case, but I wondered about the two of them. Linda didn't seem to get along with her sister at all, and that surprised me. I had always thought they had been close until Linda complained about her at the coffee shop.

She shook her head. "Annie kind of kept out of the way. She was helping Linda with different things: the meals, and cleaning the rooms, but I didn't get a chance to talk to her much. I did see the two of them arguing the night before the murder though. They were down at the end of the hall, and they weren't speaking loudly, so I didn't pick up on what was said. But I've been thinking about it, and I really don't think that anyone at the B&B could have killed that man. Everybody was friendly and having a nice stay. No one there seemed like killers."

I nodded as we headed up to the cash register. "I didn't get the feeling that anybody there could have murdered him either." Although now I was wondering about Linda. What was she nervous about? "You don't have any ideas about who could have killed him then?"

She shook her head as she placed the shoes back into the box while Lucy put her boots back on. "I don't know. I just think that somebody had to have slipped in there in the middle of the night to do it. That doesn't give me a warm fuzzy feeling, knowing they could have slipped into anyone's room. I don't know how they would have done that though because Linda does lock up the front door at night. If you want to go out for anything, she asks you to call her, and she will let you back in. But Tom and I were only interested in getting some rest. When you've got five kids, the last thing you want to do is go gallivanting around town in the middle of the night. Believe me. We don't have any interest in that." She laughed.

I smiled. "I can only imagine. Having two kids was more than enough for me, but five? I don't know if I could survive it."

"I know I couldn't," Lucy said, coming up behind us. She reached into her purse for a card to pay for the shoes. "I'm really excited about these shoes."

She nodded. "I'm going to take these to the back and treat them, and I'll be right back."

When Andrea had gone to the back, I turned to Lucy. "Why do you suppose Linda seemed so nervous?"

She shook her head. "I don't know. It was just a regular weekend, wasn't it? Sure, they were celebrating Valentine's Day, but she's done that many times since she opened the inn, I'm sure."

"Maybe she was worried about how the brunch would turn out? Maybe she hadn't gotten everything she needed or wasn't sure things would go as planned."

"That's a possibility," she said. "But she could have run to the store if she needed something. You don't think she could have killed him, do you? Why would she want to?"

"I don't know."

The last thing I wanted to do was accuse Linda. It was possible that she was anxious about the preparations for the Valentine's Day brunch, and until we found out otherwise, that was what I was going to believe.

CHAPTER 9

"How did I get so lucky to marry the most handsome man in the world?" I gazed at Alec from across the table at Antonio's, the best Italian restaurant in Maine. Alec had made reservations for us in December, and it was a good thing he did, because the place was packed with starry-eyed lovers at every table and booth. The lighting had been dimmed, and our table was covered in a red tablecloth with red and white candles in the center.

He chuckled and took a sip of his water. "I don't know. I guess some girls have all the luck."

I laughed heartily. "That's why I love you. I never know what's going to come out of your mouth."

He grinned. "I guess the same could be said about

you. And I'm feeling pretty lucky that I married the most beautiful redhead in the world."

I patted my long, curly red hair. "You are pretty lucky, aren't you?" All kidding aside, I felt fortunate to have been offered a second chance at love with a man who was as wonderful as my first husband had been. I reminded myself frequently not to take a day for granted. That lesson had been drilled into me the day the police showed up at my door to inform me that my first husband had been killed by a drunk driver.

He held up his water glass. "To us."

I clinked mine gently against his. "To us."

The waitress brought our meals out; I had ordered the lasagna a la Bolognese, and he had ordered the beef ragu, along with a bottle of expensive champagne. I rarely drank, but this was a special occasion.

Alec gazed at me after the waitress left. "There you are. A delicious Italian meal and champagne."

I nodded and cut into my lasagna with my fork. It smelled as good as I expected. I popped a bite into my mouth and almost groaned at how delicious it was. I held up my thumb and forefinger, making an 'O' to show Alec my approval without speaking with my mouth full. I didn't want to waste a moment of this bite on words.

He nodded and took a bite of his ragu, then nodded appreciatively. When he swallowed, he said,

"Excellent. I knew this place would be a good choice for Valentine's Day. Although I do feel a little guilty about not celebrating Lilly's first birthday with her."

I shook my head. "No, don't feel guilty. I told you the kids were going to have a party for her on Saturday. You can spoil her all you want then. Sarah's parents will be here too." I felt a little sorry for Sarah's parents. They lived in Wisconsin and didn't get to see the baby as often as we did. It would be nice to see them again and catch up. "How is the investigation going?"

He glanced at me. "We found the murder weapon."

I was surprised by this. I figured in the few days since the victim had been discovered, and there was no weapon found, that it wouldn't ever be found. "Where?"

"In the bushes at the house next door to the B&B. We brought in a sniffer dog, and he got interested in the bushes that separate the two houses, then he moved over to the bushes in front of the house, and it was buried under just a couple of inches of snow."

"Wow," I said, taking this in. "Did you interview the occupants of the house?"

He shook his head. "According to Linda and other neighbors, the owners are snowbirds and have been in Florida since November."

"I wonder if the killer planned to go back and retrieve it later?" I took a bite of my lasagna.

He nodded as he poured champagne into our glasses. "That's what I think. Although I don't know why they didn't already do that. We sent it to the lab to have the blood analyzed, but I'm pretty sure we know how that's going to turn out. It belongs to Paul Taylor."

I picked up my glass and took a sip. It was bubbly and delicious, just as I had hoped. "I really like champagne."

One eyebrow shot up. "Don't go getting crazy and drinking the entire bottle."

I laughed. "I will not drink the entire bottle. That would knock me out, and I'd have a headache in the morning."

He smiled and held up his champagne glass to mine. "We need to toast again. To us. To a long, healthy, beautiful life together."

I grinned. "I second that." We tapped our glasses together.

I took another bite of my dinner and glanced up just as Linda and Annie entered the restaurant. I was surprised to see them since it was Valentine's Day, and it appeared that everyone in the restaurant was with their significant other. I nudged Alec under the table with my foot and then nodded in their direction when he looked at me.

He nodded. "Well, looks like the ladies are celebrating Valentine's Day. As they should."

Linda looked in our direction and lit up with a smile. She hurried over to us, dragging her sister behind her.

"Well, fancy meeting you two here," she said, as she stopped in front of our table. "I didn't expect to see the two of you here. Isn't it lovely in here tonight? Look at all the roses and candles. They did a wonderful job decorating this place."

"Didn't they though?" I said. "It's a surprise seeing the two of you tonight. How are you doing? I know you must still be in shock over what happened at the B&B on Sunday."

Linda nodded sadly while Annie straightened her black cardigan sweater. "It certainly was a shock," Linda said, nodding. She turned to Alec. "But I sure am glad that you're on the case, Alec. I know you're going to find whoever killed poor Paul Taylor."

Alec nodded. "I assure you, I will find the killer."

"I'm so glad you're on the case," she repeated. "Alec, when are you going to make an arrest? Certainly, you've got to have a suspect, don't you? I was just telling Annie before we left the house that I was certain you had somebody in mind as the killer," she said and turned to her sister. "Didn't I just say that, Annie?"

Annie nodded and pushed her glasses up on her nose. "She did."

"I'm not at liberty to talk about suspects," Alec said.

Linda's eyes widened slightly. "So you do have somebody in mind. I knew it. I can hardly wait for you to make an arrest so we'll all be safer in this town."

"You don't have to worry about a thing," I said. "Alec will find the killer."

She nodded again. She was wearing her tan puffy coat and carrying a black handbag. "As long as the killer is arrested, that's all that matters. I don't know why you couldn't tell me who you have in mind, though. You know I am doing everything possible to help you catch the killer—I've talked to everyone I know. You might need more help from me, and I would surely give it to you."

Alec leaned back in his chair. "Like I said, I'm not at liberty to give out names. Just be assured that the killer will be caught."

She looked from him to me and then back again. "Well, certainly finding the murder weapon has to have helped. I'm sure there were fingerprints all over the handle. I can't believe it has been sitting there under those bushes all this time, and no one saw it before today."

Alec sighed. "Yes, well, it's a good thing we brought the dog in. Although someone probably would have found it when the snow melted."

She shook her head. "I don't know about that. Virginia and Franklin rarely do yard work. That knife might have lain there for years." She chuckled. "Their yard is such a mess."

"Well then, it's good we brought the dog in," he said.

Annie didn't seem to be paying much attention to the conversation but was looking around the restaurant. "Annie, that's a lovely black cardigan you're wearing," I said.

She turned to me and smiled. "Thank you. Linda gave it to me for Christmas. I told her we shouldn't be here tonight because everybody is here on a date."

"Nonsense!" Linda exclaimed. "It's Valentine's Day, and we have just as much right to celebrate it as anyone else. What difference does it make that we don't have dates? It doesn't make any difference whatsoever, and I intend to enjoy a good meal." She turned back to Alec. "Well, we don't mean to interrupt your dinner, but I certainly do hope that you make an arrest soon, Alec. Come on, Annie."

"Goodbye, ladies," I called after them. When they

were out of earshot, I looked at Alec questioningly. "What do you make of that? She sure is interested in the details of the case."

He shook his head. "She didn't seem happy about me not telling her who my list of suspects was."

"Do you have a list of suspects?"

He shrugged. "Not really. I have some people I'm keeping an eye on, but I wouldn't say they were bona fide suspects."

"I bet you just added somebody else to your list of people to keep an eye on."

He chuckled and cut into his dinner. "I just might have."

Maybe Linda's interest was normal. The victim had been found in her B&B, after all. But I couldn't help but feel she had a greater interest in who Alec might arrest than she should.

CHAPTER 10

I couldn't imagine Linda Greenwood having anything to do with the murder. And if she did, why would she kill Paul Taylor? But what was behind her nervousness the day the body was found? Was it just the fact that she was hosting a Valentine's Day brunch at her B&B? It was certainly possible, but something felt off.

The day after Valentine's Day, I headed out to the Cup and Bean Coffee Shop to pick up a Cherry Bomb Mocha. The flavor would be rotated out soon now that Valentine's Day was over, and I really enjoyed that drink. I had tried rousing Lucy, but apparently, she had made good on her plans to celebrate Valentine's Day herself and had consumed a couple of bottles of red wine last night. She mumbled into the phone and informed me it didn't look as if she was going to get out of bed before noon today. Maybe later. Lucy rarely drank, but when she did, she enjoyed herself.

I waved at Mr. Winters who was sitting at the corner table and got at the end of the short line behind a woman wearing a heavy gray wool coat who was rifling through the purse on her shoulder. There were two other customers in front of her, so I gazed at the menu board as I waited. The Chocolate Cherry Muffin was delicious, and I thought I would grab one of those along with the mocha.

There was a crash in front of me, and I realized that the woman in the wool coat had dropped a small change purse, and coins scattered on the floor beside her. "Oh, shoot!" she said. "I can't believe I'm so clumsy."

I knelt to help her pick up her change as she scrambled after a few quarters that rolled a few feet away. "I'll help you."

She glanced at me, her prematurely white hair done in a short bob, and she smiled. "Oh, you don't have to do that. Sometimes I am the clumsiest person." She shook her head in disgust.

"Oh, it's no problem," I said as I scooped up coins from the coffee shop floor. "We'll get this cleaned up in no time."

She nodded as she grabbed the errant quarters and moved back toward me. "I tell you, change gathers up at the bottom of my purse so fast, so I thought getting a small coin purse would help with the problem. But it doesn't help when you drop it on the floor at the coffee shop."

I looked up at her when her voice cracked on the last word. "It happens. It's not a big deal. We'll get these picked right up. I don't think I know you, do I? Are you from around here?"

She stuffed a handful of coins back into the purse and looked at me, shaking her head. "No, I'm not from around here. I'm from New Hampshire."

My heart skipped a beat when I heard New Hampshire. Wasn't that where Paul Taylor was from? "Oh? Are you visiting someone here?"

I kept an eye on her as her face suddenly crumpled, and she shook her head, looking away from me. "No."

"Oh, I'm so sorry," I said, and my heart broke for her. "My name is Allie Blanchard. Is there something I can help you with?"

She turned back to me, tears in her eyes. "Blanchard?"

I nodded. "Yes."

"As in Detective Alec Blanchard's wife?"

I nodded again. "Yes, he's my husband."

Her face crumpled again. "My husband is—or was —Paul Taylor."

"Oh, I'm so sorry. Please accept my condolences. Let me buy you a cup of coffee, you poor thing. We'll sit and talk for a few minutes if you'd like."

The other two people at the counter moved aside, having gotten their order, and we scooted up as we finished picking up all the coins. "Oh, that's unnecessary," she said.

"No, I insist. What would you like? Do you want something to eat?"

She looked up at the menu board, but I could tell she was still trying to keep from falling apart. "How about a Raspberry White Chocolate Mocha, medium? And a raspberry scone. But you really don't have to do this. I can pay for it."

I reached over and squeezed her arm, shaking my head. "No, I insist. I'm going to pay for your order." I looked up at the barista. "I would also like a Cherry Bomb Mocha and a Chocolate Cherry Muffin, please. And ring both orders together."

She nodded and got to work on the order, and I turned to Mrs. Taylor. "What was your name?"

"Deanna Taylor. I still can't get over that this has happened. Your husband has been so nice, as has everyone at the police department. I just don't understand what happened. Why would someone kill my husband?"

I nodded and patted her arm. "I can imagine that this must be so horrible. I lost my first husband to a drunk driver who hit his car. It's not quite the same, but it's similar."

Her face softened, and she nodded. "Yes, it's similar."

We got our coffees and food, and we went to the opposite corner from where Mr. Winters was sitting. He looked at me expectantly, and I gave him a slight shrug as we sat down. "Will you be in town long?" I asked.

She sighed. "For at least a few days. Maybe longer. I haven't decided yet."

"Do you mind me asking what Paul was doing here in town?" I wanted to ask why he had come up on Valentine's weekend and stayed at a romantic B&B when he was alone, but I left that out. Her eyes suggested she knew what day of the month it was, and she had probably been to the B&B to collect his things.

"His great-aunt passed away, and he was settling the estate. She had a house over on Grand Avenue."

I nodded. Alec had already told me he was settling the estate, but I was hoping she would mention something that might be useful in the investigation. "That's right, my husband mentioned his aunt was Daisy Taylor. I knew her. She was a very sweet woman."

She smiled. "Wasn't she, though? I was sorry that she passed, but she was 102, so I suppose it was her time." She took a sip of her coffee and nodded. "This is delicious."

"They have great coffee here. I'm so sorry about your husband."

She looked at me. "I told him not to come this weekend. It's Valentine's Day, after all." She rolled her eyes. "And then he goes and books a room at a romantic B&B." She shook her head. "That was Paul. He didn't have a romantic bone in his body and couldn't imagine why that would be seen as a little odd. But apparently, the one little motel in town was already booked, and the larger one was recently bought and was closed due to extensive renovations. He didn't want to get a room in Bangor and then drive over here, especially with all the snow. I suppose I could have come with him, but I knew he was going to be busy with the house and making phone calls. The lawyer handling the estate is an old friend."

I nodded. "I can see where that would make perfect sense to a man who isn't the least bit romantic." I chuckled. "My best friend's husband is the same way. He couldn't imagine why he should do something nice for his wife on Valentine's Day. But other than that, he's a good guy."

She nodded. "Paul was, too. He did not have a sense of humor at all, but he was a stickler for doing the right thing at all times, and I really appreciated that in him." She looked up at me. "I can't imagine who would want to kill him. There's no reason for it, unless," she hesitated and took another sip of her coffee.

"Unless what?" I prodded.

"Unless it was his nephew. His nephew was angry that he didn't get a larger piece of the inheritance from Daisy. But he didn't have any right to a larger piece of the inheritance. He lived half a mile away from her and never went to visit her. He never did anything for her, didn't even shovel the snow off her walk. The poor thing was out there doing it herself until she was ninety-eight."

I shook my head. "Really? She was doing it herself at ninety-eight?"

She nodded. "She probably would have done it up until the day she died, but she got some new neighbors who took over the job for her. Paul kept telling Jordan that he needed to get over there and get it done for her, but he refused. Over the years, we would hire somebody to shovel her snow, but for one reason or another, they always stopped doing it. I don't know, maybe she told them to stop. She was a very independent woman. Thank goodness for her new neighbors."

I nodded. "I can see that in her. I didn't realize she was shoveling her own snow, though. That's really too much work for a woman her age."

She nodded. "I agree."

"So, you think Jordan did it? Do you think he would be angry enough to kill Paul over the inheritance? And what would it change if he killed him? It wouldn't get him more of her estate, would it?"

"He thinks Paul wormed his way into the largest portion of the inheritance, by convincing her to give him less. And she was indeed leaving Paul most of her money, but he did the most for her. He called her every week to check on her, and he would make trips down here to visit her. Jordan couldn't be bothered to go half a mile for her. He, our son Eric, and my husband were Daisy's only relatives who were still in her life. Daisy did leave a small amount of money to me and to Jordan's wife, Alicia, but most of it went to Paul. So Jordan will get more money with Paul dead."

I shook my head. "That's terrible. This Jordan—is he Jordan Taylor? Works as the produce manager at the grocery store?"

She nodded. "Yes, that's him. I suppose living in a small town, everyone knows everyone else."

"Yes, exactly."

She took a sip of her coffee. "Jordan is bitter about the inheritance. So is his wife Alicia. Very bitter."

"Some people can be so ungrateful."

I knew Jordan, and I was going to have a talk with him.

CHAPTER 11

It was the following day when Lucy and I stopped by Jordan Taylor's house. If what Deanna had said about Jordan being bitter about the inheritance was true, then I wanted to see if we could get any information out of him.

I knew Taylor, but I didn't know his wife very well, and when I spotted a car in the driveway, I decided to take a chance. I had made strawberry cupcakes the day before and thought I would bring some over to them.

"These cupcakes smell so good," Lucy said as we stood on the porch, waiting for someone to answer the door.

"Thanks. That's the recipe I used for Lilly's smash cake." I'd baked the cakes for her party and popped them into the freezer until I was ready to frost them for the party. The cupcakes were a bonus.

When the door opened, Jordan's wife looked first surprised to see us and then confused. "Yes? Can I help you?"

I smiled for all I was worth. I needed to get inside to talk to her. "Good morning. Is Jordan home?"

Her brow furrowed. "Jordan? Why?"

I held up the box of cupcakes. "I'm so sorry, we don't mean to impose. I was hoping Jordan would be home. I knew his great Aunt Daisy, and I just heard that she passed away. She was such a sweet woman, and I knew he must be missing her, so I made some strawberry cupcakes and brought them by. My name is Allie Blanchard, and this is my friend Lucy Gray. I think I've seen you at the craft store."

"Hello," Lucy said, smiling. "Daisy was a sweet woman. I'm so sorry for your loss."

She seemed to relax now and nodded. "Oh, yes, poor Aunt Daisy. She was the sweetest woman ever. I still can't believe that she made it to 102. She was in such good health. I told my husband that I thought she might make it to 110, but the poor thing just didn't quite make it."

I nodded. "She was the sweetest woman. She always seemed so happy and full of energy. Well, I guess as much energy as a 102-year-old woman can muster. But she didn't use a walker or a cane, and you're right, I would have sworn she would have made it a few more years."

"She really was the sweetest person," Lucy echoed. "Isn't your name Alicia? I've talked to you at the craft store, too."

Alicia brightened. "You bought some green yarn for a knitting project a couple of weeks ago, didn't you?"

Lucy chuckled. "Sure did. And someday I'll get to it, too."

Alicia laughed.

"So anyway, I was doing a little baking and thought I would bring some cupcakes by. Jordan wouldn't happen to be home, would he?" I asked.

She shook her head, her blond hair bouncing with the movement. "No, he's at work. That was sweet of you to think of us and make some cupcakes. Would you like to come in for coffee? We could have a cupcake."

I nodded, trying not to seem too eager. "That would be wonderful." We followed her into the house and into her kitchen. It was decorated in a light blue with yellow flowers on the dish towels and the tile backsplash. "You have such a darling kitchen."

She looked over her shoulder at me. "Thank you. I

am a sucker for pastels, and I wanted my kitchen to be charming and relaxing. I'll just get us some coffee."

"I think you hit the nail on the head with the color scheme," Lucy said. "Is there something we can help you with?" she asked as Alicia got to work pouring coffee for us.

She shook her head. "No, you have a seat. It'll just take me a minute to get everything on the table. You ladies stopping by just gave me an excuse to cheat on my diet." She laughed.

I chuckled. "Well, then I've done my good deed for the day."

She laughed louder as she brought two cups of coffee over and set them in front of us, then hurried to the refrigerator to get the cream, and set it next to the sugar bowl on the table. "There. Help yourselves." She grabbed a cup of coffee for herself and returned to sit down.

I nodded as I stirred sugar into my coffee. "Don't mind if I do." I looked at her as she opened the box of cupcakes and smiled. "Alicia, how are things going with Daisy's estate, if you don't mind me asking? Did you get her house cleared out?"

She glanced at me. "Well, I hate to say it, but Daisy was a bit of a collector. And by collector, I mean a packrat," she chuckled. "The poor thing. She loved little knickknacks and crocheted doilies. Lots of knickknacks and doilies."

"Oh, my," I said, setting my coffee cup down on the table. "It sounds like you all have a lot to do in that house, then."

She sighed. "I'm glad her things brought her joy while she was alive, but it is a lot for us to go through. So, so much stuff to go through." She shook her head.

"I hope you don't have to do it all yourself," I said as I passed her the box of cupcakes.

She rolled her eyes. "I'm afraid Jordan and I got stuck with most of it. His uncle is handling the legal side of it, but we are stuck with cleaning out the house. Or I guess I should say his uncle *was* handling the legal side of it. I suppose you already know that somebody murdered him last weekend."

I nodded. "We did hear that and I'm so sorry he was murdered. My husband is the detective handling the case, and it was just so sad to hear he had been murdered."

She nodded without looking at me and took a sip of her coffee. "Yes, well, Jordan's family are all odd. And Paul was probably the worst."

"Oh?" I asked.

She helped herself to a cupcake and passed the box to Lucy. "Paul was just weird. He had no sense of humor, and it was hard to read him. He thought he was handsome and a ladies' man, but believe me, he was anything but. He even had the nerve to flirt with me occasionally—or at least I think that's what he was trying to do."

"Really?" I said, trying to sound shocked.

She nodded. "None of the family can get along with each other. There are more family members in other states, but there was a big blowout years ago, and the only people we see anymore were Daisy and Paul, his wife Deanna, and their son Eric. Honestly, I have met some of the others, and I am glad they don't come around."

"That much trouble?" I asked.

She nodded. "Yes, believe me, we're better off without them. One or the other of them was always starting arguments about something, and if they ever borrowed money from you, you could kiss it good-bye. Several of them have police records. I could go on and on."

Lucy shook her head. "There's nothing like troublesome relatives to make your life miserable."

"It sounds like you're better off without them," I said, taking a sip of my coffee and then gazing at Alicia. "Say, Alicia, do you have any idea who might have wanted to kill Paul?"

She wrapped her hands around her coffee cup and looked me dead in the eye. "Sure. His wife, Deanna."

I was stunned to hear this. When I spoke to Deanna, I thought she was sincere being the grieving widow. "Why do you say that?"

She took a moment to gather her thoughts, and then she said, "The two of them were on rocky ground, if you know what I mean."

I shook my head. "No, I don't know what you mean."

She picked up a cupcake. "Their marriage was on the rocks, is what I mean. Deanna wanted a divorce. She told Paul that she was going to take him to the cleaners, and he was going to be sorry he hadn't made her happier. She's a piece of work." She peeled the cupcake liner back. "I know you're married to the detective. You need to tell him to look into her story. She seems sweet and innocent, but that isn't her at all. She's devious. I finally had to demand that we not have holidays with them anymore, because I would have panic attacks in the days leading up to the holidays because of the way she is. Just very underhanded and controlling."

I shook my head, trying to take this in. "Really?"

She nodded. "She once told my husband I was cheating on him. When I confronted her, she laughed about it. It's hard for me to reconcile the sweet side of her with the twisted side. Honestly, if I were a betting woman, I would put my money on her as the killer."

"Really?" Lucy said, drawing the word out.

She nodded and took another sip of her coffee. "Yes. She's an awful, spiteful woman, and she couldn't wait to be done with Paul."

"I had no idea," I said, hoping she would continue. This didn't sound like the woman I had met at all.

"I'm sure she told the police she was at home in New Hampshire at the time of the murder, but it's not true." She sat up straight. "She was here in Maine."

"Did you see her?" I asked.

She glanced at me. "Sort of. She posted a video on social media on Saturday saying she was shoveling snow and running errands for the day."

My coffee was getting cold, but I didn't care. This was getting interesting. "Wait, I don't understand. If she's shoveling snow, presumably at her home, how could she be in Maine?"

She flashed me a sly smile. "Deanna is an attention seeker. She's constantly posting photos and videos of everything she does, no matter how mundane. And when she said she was out running errands, she did a quick ten-second video of her saying she was getting ready to go to lunch. But the funny thing is that she didn't show the restaurant that she was headed to, and she always does that. She wants to make sure everybody knows that she's got money to eat out all the time." She rolled her eyes. "But for a brief second, the sign at the front of the restaurant can be seen. It's Dodgers."

For a moment, I wasn't getting what she was saying.

Then Lucy gasped. "Dodgers' only has three restaurants, and they're here in Maine, isn't that right? They don't have restaurants in New Hampshire, do they?"

She shook her head conspiratorially. "No. They only have the three restaurants and they're here in Maine. There's one over in Bangor on W. Brook Ave."

It was my turn to gasp. "She was here in Maine on Saturday." I wasn't sure what to do with this information. I was going to tell Alec, of course, but in my mind, Deanna was the grieving widow, and my heart had gone out to her. But now it looked like there was proof that Deanna was here on Saturday, the day before her husband was murdered. "Can I see that video?"

She nodded and left the room. Lucy and I looked at each other.

"I can't believe it," she whispered. "Deanna lied?"

I shrugged. I had told Lucy about running into Deanna at the coffee shop, and Lucy was quite regretful that she hadn't come along with me so she could meet her. Maybe this was why Alec said she didn't seem too surprised when he called to tell her that her husband had been murdered. Because she was the killer.

Alicia returned with her phone, and she flipped through it until she found what she was looking for. She turned the phone to me, and Lucy hurried over to my side of the table as the video played. As Alicia said, Deanna announced she was running errands, and that she was stopping for lunch. The video was brief, and in the background was a small café, and for a quick fraction of a second, a green sign could be seen. But I couldn't read that sign. I didn't know which restaurant it was. "Are you sure that's Dodgers?"

She nodded. "I know it's Dodgers. My husband and I eat there regularly, and you can tell by the font they use on that sign. Watch." She started the video again, and it quickly played, but I wasn't any more convinced this time around than the first.

I looked up at her. "I don't know. It's really hard to tell from that quick glimpse."

She nodded knowingly. "Oh, believe me, it's Dodgers. She was here in Maine. She has always been such a hateful woman, and Paul put up with a lot from her. Not that he was a nice person himself, because he wasn't. He was a cheat."

"Did you show it to Alec? The video?" I asked.

She shook her head. "No, I just saw it this morning. I haven't been online for a few days because I've been very busy at work. But when I signed on this morning, that video popped up almost immediately."

"What you need to do is show the police," Lucy said. "They'll be able to examine it and determine whether it really is Dodgers."

She took a deep breath. "It is Dodgers. I'm quite certain of it. But I will call the police today."

I sat back in my seat, taking this all in. I didn't want to believe that Deanna was the heartless killer Alicia was describing, but I didn't know the woman. I suppose she could be capable of anything.

CHAPTER 12

The front door slammed, and I looked up at the clock on the wall. We had overstayed our welcome, and I was embarrassed to see it. We had been here talking to Alicia for an hour and a half. Before I could say anything, her husband, Jordan, stood in the kitchen doorway. His eyes widened, then his brow furrowed in confusion.

I smiled. "Oh, Jordan, hello. How are you doing? I haven't seen you around town in a while."

He smiled back, still looking uncertain. His eyes went to his wife, then came back to me. "Oh hey, Allie. Lucy. I've been around. I'm doing good. How are you ladies doing?"

I nodded. "We're good. We stopped by to say hello and brought some cupcakes." I nodded at the box. We each had eaten one, but there were plenty left. "I heard your great Aunt Daisy had passed away, and I felt remiss in not stopping by and paying our respects."

"I was so sad to hear that she had died," Lucy said. "She was such a wonderful woman, and this town will be poorer for not having her around."

He seemed to relax now, and he nodded. "Yes, we were surprised that Aunt Daisy passed away when she did." Then he seemed to rethink his words. "I mean, obviously at 102, it shouldn't be a surprise, but still. We figured she'd be around for at least a few more years."

Alicia smiled at her husband. "I was just telling the ladies how sorry we all were for her passing. Aunt Daisy was a sweetie."

He nodded. "Yes, she certainly was."

"You should try one of my cupcakes," I said, nodding at the box again. "They're strawberry. I was working on my recipe for my granddaughter's first birthday cake, and when I heard about your aunt, I decided I should make you some cupcakes and bring them by. We really are sorry for your loss."

He nodded and went to the coffeepot and poured himself a cup. "I think a strawberry cupcake sounds delicious, and I'm starving. I skipped breakfast."

"Oh, then you're in luck," Lucy said. "There's nothing like something sweet for breakfast."

He chuckled and came over and sat next to his wife, glancing at her. "I don't go to work until later, and I was out running errands."

She nodded and something seemed to pass between them. "We were just talking about how wonderful Aunt Daisy was and how we'll miss her."

He turned to us. "Yeah, we sure are going to miss Aunt Daisy. She was such a wonderful person."

"I bet it's going to leave an enormous hole in your life," Lucy said. "I really enjoyed talking to her whenever I ran into her around town. She was always so active in community events, and I saw her out and about frequently."

"She was a real go-getter." He chuckled. "She always insisted on doing so much for herself. I mean, we were over at her house helping her all the time. You know, yard work, helping her clean her house, shoveling snow. Just whatever she needed to do around the house. But she always insisted that she didn't need the help."

I was surprised by this since Deanna had said Jordan was lazy and wouldn't help his aunt at all. "I bet that was a lot of work on top of doing things like that around your own house and also going to work."

He smiled. "Oh, yeah, but you know how it is.

When you've got somebody in your life who is just so sweet, like my great aunt was, you don't hesitate to help. Plus, even though she was active, she still needed a lot of help with things around the house."

"I took her shopping every week," Alicia added. "She gave up driving, and there was no way I was going to allow her to take public transit for grocery shopping. Especially during the winter. But it was no trouble. I enjoyed it."

"I bet you did," I said, smiling. "Daisy was a lovely person."

She turned to Jordan. "We were also talking about how sad it was about Paul."

He poured cream into his cup and stirred, nodding. "Yeah, that was a shock." He looked at us. "I never in a million years would have thought somebody would murder him like that. It's just, I don't know, weird."

I nodded and took a sip of my now cold coffee. "And of all places for it to happen. At a romantic B&B on the weekend before Valentine's Day. It's just so unusual."

He gave a curt nod of his head and reached for a cupcake. "This sure looks good. Yeah, that was weird, being Valentine's weekend. Does your husband have any idea who might have killed him?"

I gave a quick shake of my head. "Not yet. These

investigations can take some time, but I know he'll find the killer soon. You don't have any idea who might have wanted to kill him?"

He hesitated, then took a large bite of the cupcake and nodded appreciatively. When he swallowed, he said, "This cupcake is delicious. Allie, I don't know how you bake so well, but this is incredibly good. I've sampled some of your work in the past, but I think this might be the best strawberry cupcake I've ever eaten."

I smiled, noting the fact that he didn't answer my question. "Thank you, Jordan. I certainly do appreciate hearing when somebody enjoys my baked goods. I work hard to make sure they are the best they can be, and nothing makes me happier than to hear how much somebody enjoys them."

"Nobody bakes better than Allie," Lucy said. "I'm jealous of her talent."

I smiled at Lucy. "Oh, Lucy, you are the biggest help when I have a large job, and you are a great apprentice."

She laughed. "I didn't realize I was your apprentice. I like that title."

I turned back to the two of them, and they were looking at one another. "I have to wonder about Paul, though. Alicia said she thinks his wife was in town." Never mind the fact that I had run into her and spoken to her myself. Something was going on between the two of them, and I wanted to know what it was.

Jordan frowned. "Yeah, I'm sure she's here in town. I haven't spoken to her, and I don't intend to. I've never liked her, and I wouldn't trust her as far as I could throw her."

"Oh?" I asked. "You didn't care for her?"

He nodded and took a sip of his coffee. "She's a hateful woman. Controlling and always got her nose in everybody else's business. I don't like her." He chuckled, but it sounded hollow. "Maybe I sound terrible. I don't know. But ever since Paul married her, it was like the family kind of fell apart. Nobody was as close as they had once been, and it was because she drove a wedge between everyone."

"That must have been very difficult for you all. I wonder what would make her want to do that?" I could not reconcile the picture he and Alicia were painting of Deanna with the woman I had met at the coffee shop.

He shrugged. "I don't know. I think some people are just that way. It's like they're miserable, so they need to make everybody else miserable."

"Oh, I know what the reason was," Alicia said knowingly. "It was money. She wanted Aunt Daisy's money. She wanted to move back here to Sandy

Harbor so that she could be the person who helped out with Aunt Daisy. I think she felt like that would entitle her to more of her money when she finally did pass away."

"Oh, that's terrible," Lucy said. "She just wanted to be close to her so she could make sure she got some of her money?"

She nodded. "As it was, Paul finagled the lion's share of the inheritance. I can imagine if they had moved back to town, and she had gone through the motions of taking care of Aunt Daisy—they probably would have ended up with all the money." She made a face and took a sip of her coffee, then set the cup back on the table. "Some people are just awful, and there's nothing you can do about it."

Jordan nodded. "You can say that again. It wasn't right that Paul got Aunt Daisy to sign over so much of her money into his name. He knew it wasn't right, and he lied about us to her to get her to do it, too." He suddenly stood up. "Well, if you ladies will excuse me, I've got some things to take care of around the house before I go back to work."

I nodded. "Of course, Jordan. We didn't mean to keep you this long. We had better get going, too." I looked at Lucy, and we both stood up.

"Oh, it's no trouble. I don't get visitors very often, so it was nice to sit and talk. Thank you again for these cupcakes." Alicia got up and walked us out to the door.

When we were back in my car, I turned to Lucy. "What they said is the exact opposite of what Deanna told me. She said that they refused to help Daisy with anything."

She nodded. "To be honest, I felt like they were trying to hide something."

I agreed. And I was going to find out what that something was.

CHAPTER 13

"How are you doing, Allie?" Emily Stone asked me as she scooped me up into a hug.

"I'm doing great. It's so good to see you, Emily," I said, hugging her, and then hugging her husband, Bert. Emily and Bert were Sarah's parents, and they were here for the weekend for Lilly's first birthday. I was ecstatic about this party, and I couldn't wait to see what Lilly would do with her smash cake. Smash it, hopefully.

"Alec, how are you doing?" Bert asked as Alec carried the birthday cake in. Jennifer was behind him with a smaller box holding the smash cake.

Alec nodded and smiled. "I'm doing well, Bert. Yourself?"

He nodded. "I'm ready to see our baby girl celebrate her first birthday, so I'm doing alright."

Alec grinned as he carried the cake to the kitchen. "Me too."

I turned to Emily. "How was your flight?"

She grinned. "Uneventful, just the way I like them."

I chuckled as I carried the fruit salad into the kitchen.

Sarah was running back and forth in the kitchen, making last-minute finishing touches to the food for the party. She looked harried.

"Sarah, how can I help?" I asked as I set the bowl of fruit salad on the counter.

"I'll help, too," Lucy said. "Ed might even pitch in."

Ed shrugged. "Sure."

She waved a hand at me. "Nonsense, you all are here to celebrate with Lilly. I'm taking care of everything."

"She's been like this all morning," Emily said with a sigh. "I want to help her, and she won't allow it."

"I'll help you," Jennifer said. She grabbed an apron from a nearby hook and tied it around her waist.

"Honestly, I've got everything. The burgers are ready to be put on the grill, the potato salad is done, and there are hors d'oeuvres, and chips and dip to be set out on the table. Honestly, I kept it simple. A couple of friends from work are going to be here with their kids, but it will be mainly us adults." She stopped and sighed. She wasn't fooling me; she was frazzled. First birthdays will do that to you. Everything has got to be perfect, or at least that's what we tell ourselves.

"I brought a fruit salad, and I can whip up anything you need me to," I offered.

"I can help," her mother said.

Lucy nodded. "Me too."

Sarah sighed. "Honestly, I think I've got everything. Thad cleared the snow from the patio and is working on the barbecue, and once that's done, we'll eat. But I'm still waiting for a couple of people."

The doorbell rang then, and her dad said, "I'll get it," and headed to the front door.

Sarah looked at us. "I think this party is going to be a flop. I just know it."

I shook my head. "What are you talking about? It's your baby's first birthday; just relax. Everything is going to be great."

She sighed. "I don't know if I can. Honestly. I feel like I'm forgetting something."

"Ed, let's go out and see what Thad is up to," Alec said and they skedaddled out of the kitchen when it appeared that Sarah might break down into tears. That one wasn't much on comforting crying women.

I went to the refrigerator and looked inside. "Okay, I see you've got iced tea and lemonade. Perfect. Let me put a tray together with the trimmings for the burgers."

"Thank you, Allie," Sarah relented, and she went back to working on the deviled eggs.

Emily opened a cupboard. "There's a relish tray here we can use," she said, pulling it from the cupboard and bringing it to the kitchen island. "We'll have everything set up and ready to go. This party is going to be a breeze."

I winked at her. This year had been a first for everything Lilly had accomplished, but it had also been a year full of firsts for Sarah. It was her first birth, her first time as a mother, her first time breastfeeding, changing diapers, and somehow managing a career at the same time. The poor girl was worn out.

I got some lettuce and tomatoes from the refrigerator and set them on the island, then got some purple onions and set them there, too. Next, I pulled out mayonnaise, ketchup, mustard, barbecue sauce, and anything else I could think of that would go with burgers. I looked at Sarah. "Oh, I know, I can whip up some barbecue beans really quick if you have some plain canned beans. It won't take me but a minute."

She turned to me. "Baked beans would be a

fantastic side for the burgers. Why didn't I think of that?" she groaned. "This is going to be a mess."

Jennifer went to her cupboard and began looking for the beans.

"Stop saying that," I said mildly. "This is going to be a happy day. And where is the baby?" I turned to look for her. In the rush to help Sarah, I had forgotten to ask about the baby.

"She's taking a nap. I think she sensed the excitement and got worked up, so I put her down for an early nap," Sarah said.

"That is an excellent idea," I said. "She'll be rested up for the party."

We got to work on getting the food ready as the rest of Sarah's guests arrived. She and her mother had gotten up early to decorate the house in adorable pink and white streamers and balloons, and bunnies everywhere. This was going to be fun.

"THESE BURGERS ARE DELICIOUS," I said to Thad as I sat across from him at the table. Sarah had gotten some folding tables and put them in the living room so we would have enough room to sit together.

"Thanks, Mom," Thad said. "There's nothing like a barbecue, even when it's freezing cold outside."

I laughed and took a sip of my lemonade. It was wonderful that Lilly had been born on Valentine's Day, but that meant she was always going to have her birthday parties in the winter, which could get a little tricky in Maine. Lilly was in the highchair, and I reached over and stroked her hand while she fed herself sliced bananas. "Look at our sweet girl."

"It's hard to believe she's a year old," Emily said.

I nodded. "The year flew by so fast."

Thad turned to Alec. "Alec, how is that murder case going?"

Alec nodded. "It's going."

"I heard the victim was related to Jordan Taylor?" he asked.

Alec nodded. "Yes, he was Jordan's uncle."

"Isn't Jordan your age?" I asked Thad, realizing that they probably went to school together.

He chuckled. "Yeah. He was in my graduating class. He was something else, and to be honest, I wouldn't trust him as far as I could throw him."

"Oh?" Alec asked.

He nodded. "Let's just say that Jordan was the kind of kid who always had something up his sleeve. It's like he was always looking to take advantage of any situation. He was good at flattering people, especially the teachers. That alone made me not trust him."

I wasn't sure if Thad had been on the receiving

end of some sort of scheme that Jordan had been up to back then or not. I remembered how he had praised my cupcakes. Was he just flattering me? "Did you have trouble with him?"

He shrugged. "Sort of. You probably won't remember, but in the tenth grade, I may have skipped a day of school." He looked at me, one brow raised.

"As a matter of fact, I do remember that." My kids were not troublemakers ordinarily, so when they did something out of character, it stood out.

He nodded. "He and a couple of other guys were with me. We were just playing hooky and wandering around town until it was time to go home at our normal time. But he went and snitched on us. Said he had gone to a doctor's appointment and saw us wandering around town. Of course, he had a note from his mother, so he didn't get into trouble for it."

"He sounds like a real jerk," Lucy said and took a bite of her fruit salad.

He nodded. "Oh, he's a jerk, all right. Just whatever he tells you, Alec, take it with a grain of salt."

Alec nodded. "I've talked to him twice. I don't know if he had anything to do with his uncle's murder, but he tried to sweet-talk me and make me think he was my friend."

He nodded. "Exactly. I don't know what his wife

saw in him or why she married him. She was always a sweet girl in school."

"Did Alicia graduate the same year you did?" I asked.

He nodded. "Yeah. I went out with her in the ninth grade. Don't you remember?"

I gazed at him, trying to remember, and shook my head. And then it dawned on me—Alicia had been the cute girl who had been chatty and seemed very nice when I met her. "Oh my gosh, how could I have forgotten? How long did you two go out?"

"Only three or four times, I think. She dumped me for Jordan." He rolled his eyes. "Clearly, she had no taste in guys."

Sarah laughed. "Clearly, she didn't."

I chuckled. "Her loss then."

He nodded. "She fell for his smarminess. She was always a nice girl, though."

They were an interesting couple, to be sure.

We finished up with our meal and then cleaned up and folded up the tables so there was more room in the living room for Lilly to open her presents. Thad brought her highchair in, and when she finished opening her gifts with a lot of help from her parents, we gave her the pink smash cake. In true baby fashion, she touched it with her fingers and then rubbed her fingers together when they got frosting on them.

"Come on, Lilly," Thad said. "Give it a great big smash. It will be so satisfying."

We chuckled and took pictures, and I was holding my phone so that my mother could see what was going on.

"There's my big girl," Mama said from the other end of the line, drawing Lilly's attention. She grinned when I held the phone up close so she could see her great-grandmother.

"Oh, aren't you the sweetest," Mama said. "I'm so sorry I missed your birthday, Honey, but you just wait. When I get out there to visit again, I'll make it up to you."

"We all miss you, Grandma," Sarah said as Lilly suddenly grabbed a handful of cake and held it up. We all laughed. How did I make it so many years without having a grandbaby of my own to love?

CHAPTER 14

I woke the following Monday morning to a bright, sunshiny day. I was surprised to see that I had slept in until nearly eight o'clock, but we had spent nearly the entire weekend hanging out at Thad and Sarah's apartment, visiting with them and Sarah's parents. And the best thing of all? Lilly had said 'Mimi'. I know, I know. But it wasn't my imagination this time. All the prompting I had done had finally paid off.

I hummed as I got dressed and texted Lucy, telling her I wanted to skip our morning run. We had taken to going to the gym to run on treadmills some mornings, but after having gotten up so late, I wasn't in the mood.

I couldn't get over how bright the day was as I

drove down to the Cup and Bean Coffee Shop. It was going to be a beautiful day.

Mr. Winters was sitting at his favorite table with the newspaper spread out in front of him. I gave him a little wave as I went to the counter to place my order; a mocha for Alec and a caramel latte for me. Hopefully, Alec wouldn't be too busy to talk.

Before leaving the shop, I stopped by Mr. Winters' table to say hello. "How are you doing, Mr. Winters?"

He nodded, folded his newspaper over, and tapped on the table across from him, indicating he wanted me to sit down. I dutifully did as he wanted.

"I was talking to Daisy Taylor's neighbor, Lavonne Hodges yesterday. She said that shortly before she died, Daisy told her she was worried about the pressure some of her family members were putting on her regarding her will."

"Which relatives?" I asked.

He shook his head. "Lavonne didn't know. She said that Daisy was disgusted by the whole thing. She even suggested she might just leave all her money to charity. She said that would serve them right."

I took a sip of my latte. "Well, from what I've heard, the only relatives she was in contact with were Paul, his son Eric, and Jordan Taylor. So it had to be one of them, and since Paul is dead, that leaves Jordan and Eric. But I get the sense that Eric hasn't been around much."

"Maybe. But Lavonne said Daisy referred to this relative as 'she'."

"She? Did she ask Daisy who it was? Why the secrecy?"

He shrugged. "You know Daisy. She was always so positive about everything. Maybe she didn't want to be negative about this person."

"Then if it's a 'she', it would have to be Paul's wife Deanna, or Jordan's wife, Alicia. How confident are you that Lavonne got the story right?" Neither of these two made sense. The inheritance was their husbands' business, and while they would still profit from the inheritance, maybe as much as their husbands would, would they go to the effort to put pressure on Daisy to get her to increase it? If so, then it had to be Alicia.

"She seemed positive about what she had heard, but you know Lavonne. She likes to talk a lot, and she likes to gossip."

I thought about this. "Maybe whoever it was thought that Daisy would be a soft touch because of her age."

He nodded. "That's a possibility."

"Did she say anything else?"

He shook his head. "No, that was all she knew."

"Okay, then, I'll keep it in mind. I've got to drop this mocha off to Alec before it gets cold. It's good talking to you, and I will see you later." I patted the little poodle's head beneath the table and stood up.

He nodded. "I'll expect a full report soon."

I gave him a little salute with my cup of coffee and headed out the door. This was interesting. Would Deanna have had a genuine reason to kill her husband? If so, why would she wait until he was at the B&B to do it? She could have killed him at home in New Hampshire. It didn't make sense. That left Alicia. But I couldn't see Alicia doing it.

* * *

As luck would have it, when I pulled into the parking lot at the police department, Alec was walking out the door. I parked next to his car and waved at him when he looked up. He grinned, and I got out of the car.

"You read my mind. I was just stepping out to get a cup of coffee."

When he got to me, I kissed him and handed him the coffee. "Well, I just saved you a trip. How are you doing?"

He wrapped his free arm around me and kissed me again. "I'm doing great. It was nice getting to visit with the Stones over the weekend, but I am worn out."

"Me too. There's something I have to tell you." I told him exactly what Mr. Winters had told me, and I waited for his reaction.

He nodded. "I'll keep it in mind."

Before I could say anything else, another car pulled into the parking lot and parked on the other side of my car. It was Deanna Taylor. She nodded and got out of the car when she shut the engine off. "Good morning. I hope I'm not interrupting anything."

Alec shook his head and released me. "No, we were just catching up." He took a sip of coffee. "How are you this morning?"

She nodded and came around the side of the car, and a tall young man got out of the passenger side of her car. "I'm doing well. This is my son, Eric. He came down to drive my husband's car back home."

Alec nodded and shook his hand. "Pleased to meet you. I'm sorry for your loss."

"Yes, I'm so sorry," I echoed.

He frowned and nodded. "Thank you. I don't know who killed my father, but I expect you to figure it out."

I was taken aback by his tone, and I glanced at Alec. His face was unreadable.

"We are doing everything in our power to find his killer," Alec said.

Deanna put a hand on Eric's arm. "We know that you're working to find Paul's killer, and we appreciate all the hard work you're putting into it. Do you have any new leads?"

Alec hesitated, then shook his head. "Nothing new. We got some fingerprints back, but nothing matches anyone in the system."

She nodded. "I suppose there are lots of fingerprints in that room from prior guests. Who knows if those fingerprints belong to one of them rather than the killer?" She sighed. "They were probably wearing gloves, anyway. At least that would have been the smart thing to do if they were going to commit a crime like that."

I shot her a look. The comment struck me as odd.

Alec nodded. "Yes, that's the trouble with getting fingerprints from a place that is frequented by a variety of people. But as I said, we will find your husband's killer."

She tightened her scarf against the chilly breeze. "Well, I want to remind you again about Andersen's nephew, Jordan. He's the most likely killer."

"Yeah, I don't doubt for one minute he killed my father. He lives right down the street from that B&B, and he was angry about my father getting the larger share of my great aunt's estate. He's always been greedy. He's always complained about not making enough money and that his boss was taking advantage of him. When he found out the will had been changed, he was furious," Eric said, glancing at his mother, but she wasn't looking at him.

Alec nodded. "Yes, your mother brought all of that to my attention, and I'm certainly keeping it in mind during this investigation. He has an alibi, however; he and his wife were out to dinner."

That answer didn't seem to sit well with Eric, as his cheeks suddenly turned pink, and his jaw was set. "Just because they're backing each other up doesn't mean they have a valid alibi. You can't just take their word for it."

"I didn't say I was taking their word for it," Alec said. "I checked with the restaurant, and several people saw them there that night."

"Well, how do you know when my father was killed?" he asked. "Maybe they did it afterward."

Alec nodded. "The coroner gave me a timeframe for when he had been murdered, and the timeframe was for when they were at the restaurant. It isn't an exact science, of course; it's just a timeframe, so it's possible it could have happened earlier or later, but until I have evidence saying he killed your father, I can't arrest him."

Eric blew air out of his mouth in frustration. "I'm telling you, he is the only person who would kill my father. He's guilty, and he needs to be put behind bars before he kills somebody else." He sounded like he was on the verge of tears now.

It appeared Alicia was correct. There was a lot of tension and animosity in this family, and even the younger generation had picked up on it.

"I know Alec will find your father's killer," I said, hoping to soothe his anger. It's not like I could blame him. His father had been murdered in cold blood, and who wouldn't be angry about that?

He shot me an angry look but didn't say anything else.

"I think you're going to have to arrest him," Deanna said. "He has to be the killer. I've been thinking about it, and I think both he and his wife teamed up to do it. It makes the most sense to me."

"Why does it make sense to you?" Alec said, and to his credit, he sounded unruffled.

She shook her head. "Jordan is a terrible person. There were several times he called my husband, calling him filthy names and demanding that he get Daisy to change the will. I could hear Alicia encouraging him in the background, telling him to tell Paul they were going to get a lawyer, and they were going to sue. She said she was going to go down there and have a talk with Daisy and it worried both of us—at Daisy's age, the stress could have killed her. Paul called Daisy and told her not to listen to them and if they got nasty with her, to call the police."

"Paul told you this?" Alec asked.

She nodded. "Yes, Paul was worried they might harm Daisy because of her age. She was so frail she couldn't have done anything to protect herself."

"Did they ever threaten her?" Alec asked. "Or harm her in any way?"

She hesitated and shook her head. "No, they never did. Both Paul and I asked her about it several times, and she said that they had not."

"You said that they never helped Daisy out," I reminded her. "Not at all? Did they ever go over and help her with anything?" I didn't want to point out that they had told me they had been a big help to her. I didn't know how she would feel about me asking around.

She shook her head. "The only time they ever went over to help her is when Paul called Jordan and threatened them. In the middle of several particularly terrible snowstorms, Paul insisted they go over and shovel her walk and take her to the grocery store to make sure she had food in the house. And by 'threat-en,' I mean he told them he was going to take Daisy down to the lawyer and have Jordan completely cut out of the will."

"So they did sometimes help," I said, taking this in.

She rolled her eyes. "If that's what you want to call it."

I was having difficulty figuring out what the truth was. Had Jordan and Alicia done it willingly? Or were they now trying to say that, to make themselves look like they were eagerly helping Daisy when they had actually been coerced into doing it? Or were they threatened at all? As I looked at Deanna, I wondered what the truth was.

We talked to Deanna and Eric for a few more minutes before they left, and as they pulled out of the parking lot, I turned to Alec. "What do you think?"

He took a sip of his coffee, his eyes on the car as it drove down the street. "I think that punk better watch himself."

I chuckled and lightly punched his arm. "Be careful now. We don't want any complaints of police brutality."

"Oh, believe me, I'll make sure he doesn't have anybody to tell."

I laughed.

He leaned over and kissed me. "Thank you for the coffee, but since I don't have to make a trip to the coffee shop, I had better get back inside the station and get back to work."

I nodded and kissed him again. "You're welcome. I'll see you tonight."

"See you."

I got back into my car, thinking over the things that I knew about this case so far. Everyone's story seemed convincing, and I wasn't sure who the liar was. But one of them was indeed lying.

CHAPTER 15

Paul Taylor's murder was at the forefront of my mind as I went about my life that February. That was the thing: I was able to go about my life because I was still here, but there were people who knew and loved Paul, whose lives had stopped—at least temporarily. Not to mention Paul's life had permanently been stopped.

I took hold of Alec's hand as we headed for Stan's Crab Shack. We hadn't been here in ages, and Alec had managed to slip away from work for a quick lunch out. "I am starving," I said.

He lightly squeezed my hand. "Me too. I could go for a steaming hot bowl of clam chowder."

I chuckled to myself. I would never get over the joy of hearing him say "chowder" with his Maine accent. *Chowda*. "That sounds delicious, but I might get that steak and seafood plate that I got the last time we were here." The plate was a lunch-sized portion, with a petite sirloin steak, fried shrimp, and a couple of crab legs just for fun. A baked potato and salad rounded out the meal.

"Oh, I forgot about that. That does sound good. I might get that instead."

When we stepped into the restaurant, I was disappointed to see that people were sitting on the padded benches in the foyer waiting to be seated. I turned to him. "It might be a long wait. Can you be away from work that long?"

He glanced around at the dozen or so people sitting and visiting with one another as they waited. "I think these are really just a couple of groups of people, maybe three at the most. It may not take long."

I nodded. "If the wait is too long, we can go someplace else, though."

I went up to the hostess' station and gave her our names, and then we went back to sit on an empty bench.

"I'm starving," he said.

"Me too," I replied. I turned to him. "Anything new with the case?" I don't know how he didn't get worn out by my constant questions. Every time he came home, I asked him if he had anything new, but he was always steady and patient. The man was a saint.

He sighed and shook his head. "The coroner sent back his final reports, and there wasn't anything unusual on it. He was stabbed three times, but there was no sign of a struggle and no alcohol or drugs in his system." He looked at me. "The more I think about things, the more I believe somebody at the B&B had to have killed him. How could no one have known somebody was in his room with him when he was supposed to be alone? How could they not have heard something? Why didn't anyone hear anything?"

"Why didn't he scream?"

"Surprise. Shock. Some people don't scream," he said with a shrug.

I nodded. "Maybe it was someone at the B&B, but you didn't feel that anybody there was responsible in the beginning," I pointed out. "Nobody seemed to have a motive."

He nodded as a group of five people was called for a table and left. "None of them seem to have a motive to murder him. But that doesn't mean a motive doesn't exist."

He was right, of course. He always was. The front door was pushed open and a whoosh of cold air hit us as Linda and Annie hurried in. They let the door close behind them and stopped to look at everyone waiting. When they saw us, they both waved, and I waved back.

"Oh dear, I hope there's not a long wait time," Linda said as she hurried to the hostess station to leave her name.

Annie sidled up to us. "How goes it, folks?"

I smiled. "It goes great. How about you, Annie?"

She nodded. "Just fine and dandy. The seafood smells so good in here."

Linda waved Annie over and they sat on the bench that the group of people had just vacated. Linda smiled at me, and I smiled back. The door opened again, and we were hit with another whoosh of cold air. We hadn't chosen the best place to sit. Deanna and her son hurried through the door and up to the hostess station without looking in our direction.

I glanced at Alec. He had caught sight of them as well.

I glanced over at Linda. She had already struck up a conversation with a woman sitting next to her. After a few moments, they were deep in conversation about her B&B.

When Deanna turned to find a place to sit, she suddenly zeroed in on Linda as she spoke animatedly with the woman beside her about her B&B.

"Excuse me," Deanna interrupted, moving closer

to her. "Did I hear you say something about the B&B here in town?"

Linda smiled, probably thinking that she might be able to rustle up some business with this woman. "Yes, I own the Bluebell Bed and Breakfast. We serve the freshest food around and offer a quiet, romantic getaway at a reasonable price. I have a business card if you would like one."

I watched as Deanna clenched her fist at her side. "A business card?" Her tone was incredulous.

Linda nodded and quickly fished one out of her purse, and stood up, stretching her hand out with the business card. "Here you are. I don't think I got your name, but my name is Linda Greenwood, and we would be most happy if you ever chose to stay with us."

I nudged Alec, but there was no reason to do it. His eyes were on the women.

"Tell me, are there other B&Bs in this town?" Deanna asked.

Linda shook her head. "Oh, no. My B&B is the only one for miles around. Believe me, you can't get better service in a larger town than what we provide right here in Sandy Harbor."

"My husband died in your B&B." Deanna's face turned pink, and her son stepped closer to her.

Linda's mouth dropped open. It took her a few

moments to regain her composure. "Oh. Oh, dear. I am so sorry for your loss. It was a terrible, terrible thing that happened. I don't know who did it or how it could have even happened since the B&B was locked up when everyone went to bed. But I know that the police are looking into it." She nodded at Alec. "There's the lead detective now. I am sure if you have any questions, he would be more than happy to answer them."

Deanna inhaled deeply before saying anything more. "I am sure that he would. But you're Linda Greenwood. I know who you are."

That was an odd thing to say. I turned and looked at Alec, but his eyes were still on the women.

Linda shook her head. "What are you talking about? I just told you my name and I handed you a business card, but you act as if you already knew my name." She looked at me helplessly and then turned back to Deanna.

"Because I know about you and my husband. Did you really think I wouldn't find out about you?"

Linda went pale. "I'm sorry, I don't know what you're talking about. Maybe you're confusing me with someone else."

Deanna took two menacing steps closer to Linda, who looked appalled that she had decreased the distance between them.

"I found your love letters to my husband among his things last year. Did you really think that I wouldn't find out?"

It seemed as if every person in earshot was holding their breath, including me. I reached over and touched Alec's hand, but he ignored me.

Linda swallowed. "I don't know what you're talking about. I don't know who has been filling your head with lies, but I didn't know your husband before he showed up at the B&B. He was, and is, a stranger to me."

"I thought he looked familiar," Annie said.

Linda whipped around to look at her sister. "Shut up. You don't know what you're talking about. I never laid eyes on that man before he showed up to rent the room."

Deanna suddenly lunged at Linda, but her son was fast, and he grabbed her around the waist, pulling her back. "I hate you!" Deanna shouted, along with a few other unsavory words. She fought to get out of Eric's grip.

Alec was on his feet in a flash and stood between Deanna and Linda. "No, Deanna, don't do this. I don't want to have to take you to jail."

Deanna suddenly seemed to come to herself, and she shook her head. "She was having an affair with my husband. She killed him. I thought it was his nephew, but I didn't know she owned the B&B that he died in. She's his killer."

"It's a lie," Linda said, stepping out of Deanna's reach as she took a swipe at her. "I don't know what she's talking about."

Alec glanced at Linda and turned back to Deanna. "Deanna, you don't want me to have to take you to jail. You need to calm down."

She nodded, her cheeks red with anger. "All right then. But she killed my husband. Aren't you going to arrest her?"

Alec looked at Linda reluctantly. "I think it would be good if we went downtown and had a talk, Linda."

Linda put a hand to her throat. "What? Why? I haven't done anything. You've asked me all the questions that could possibly be asked, and I answered them. Why do we need to go downtown?"

"Linda, let's go downtown," Alec said firmly. "It would be best if you go willingly."

Linda swallowed and then nodded reluctantly. "Okay. We can go downtown, but I've already told you everything that needs to be said." She turned to her sister. "Annie, you'll have to come with me since I'm driving."

"Alec can drive you to the station, Linda. Annie can take me home," I said. "If you don't mind, Annie." I was going to need a ride.

Linda sighed and held her keys out to her sister. "Fine. I'll see you this evening, Annie."

Alec and Linda left with everyone staring after them, and my name was called for a table. I stood up and looked at Annie. "Well, Annie, we may as well have lunch."

Annie nodded and stood up. "Yes, I'm starving."

I could feel the eyes of everyone in the restaurant on us, but we were hungry, and we were going to eat. It would be a while before I heard back from Alec anyway.

I WAITED ANXIOUSLY until I heard Alec at the front door. I reached for the doorknob, but he beat me to it and the door swung open. He jumped back, startled, when he saw me.

"What happened? Did she confess? She killed him, didn't she?" I said in a rush.

He shook his head, smiling. "What, no 'hello, honey'? No, 'how was your day'? Have we really been married so long that you've forgotten to consider my feelings?"

I rolled my eyes dramatically. "I'm so sorry, darling husband, how was your day? How are you? I missed you." I leaned over and pecked him on the cheek. "There. What happened? Don't leave out any details."

He chuckled and walked past me, swinging the door shut behind him. "I can't believe she just lied to my face about knowing Paul." He stripped off his overcoat and hung it in the hall closet. "Can you believe it? She lied."

I shook my head, following behind him. "No, I can't believe it. What did she say? Why did she kill him?"

He closed the hall closet door and paused. "I had to let her go."

I gasped. "What? Why?"

He looked me in the eye. "I don't have enough evidence to arrest her. She maintains that she knew him years ago. They had an affair, but it's been over for years. And when he came to town, she was hoping to rekindle that affair. She swears she didn't kill him."

I gasped again. "An affair?"

He nodded. "An affair."

I shook my head. "Then who killed him?"

He shrugged. "That's what I'd like to know."

I followed him into the kitchen, where he poured himself a cup of coffee. "I'm having a hard time knowing whether to believe her. I think she's telling the truth. But she's also my best suspect at the moment. So, if she's still lying, I need to find out."

I groaned. "I don't think Linda could have done it, but at the same time, you're right. She's our best suspect."

He turned and looked at me. "*Our* best suspect?"

I nodded. "Yes. She's our best suspect."

He chuckled and got the creamer from the refrigerator.

I didn't like thinking that Linda might be a killer, but she had lied, and she was on the premises when Paul Taylor died.

CHAPTER 16

Finding out that Linda did, in fact, know our victim, Paul Taylor, after she had lied and said she hadn't known him, was quite shocking. But learning that she had actually had an affair with him years ago was worse.

Annie and I had enjoyed a delightful seafood dinner while Linda was squirming under the bright lights of the interrogation room. Okay, I've never actually seen the interrogation room, and Alec has impressed upon me that the police do not shine bright lights into a suspect's eyes to force a confession anymore, but that doesn't mean the room is any more comfortable.

I was still stunned at the thought that Linda had an affair with Paul years ago.

The doorbell rang frantically the following morning, and I hesitated before opening it. Looking through the peephole, I saw it was none other than Linda herself. Great.

"Good morning, Linda," I said, trying to keep it light when I opened the door. "What has you up this early?" As if I didn't know.

Linda's eyes were red and swollen as if she had been up crying most of the night. "Oh, Allie, I need to speak with you. May I come in?"

I hesitated. Alec hadn't arrested her because he didn't feel he had a strong enough case against her. That didn't mean that he wouldn't arrest her at some point. How crazy would I be to allow a killer into my house? Or at least a potential killer? But this was Linda. I didn't for one minute believe Linda was a killer. Did I? I didn't want to take any chances, and I didn't want to make Alec angry. So I shook my head. "I'm sorry, Linda, but I can't do that. I don't think you should even be here."

Her eyes widened in surprise. She had obviously thought that I would let her into my home, and that made me a little worried. A large black purse was slung over her shoulder—one large enough to hold a big knife. "Oh, Allie, I couldn't kill anyone. You don't think that I could, do you?"

I smiled sympathetically. "Linda, I am not working

on this case, and my opinion doesn't make any difference."

She shook her head slowly. "Oh, but it does. It means a lot. You are a character witness. You've known me for over twenty years. And you know I could never kill anyone. You've got to tell Alec that I am innocent."

I closed my eyes just for a moment and held back a sigh. "But Linda, I really can't get involved in this. Why did you tell Alec that you didn't know Paul when we found him dead in your B&B?"

She sighed. "We had an affair years ago—well, over ten years ago. So what difference would it make now? It's not my fault that he ended up dead in my B&B, and, well, I don't know. It just didn't want to muddy the waters, so to speak."

I nodded. "Because you were worried that Alec was going to look at you with interest as a suspect." That was the bottom line. She was afraid that she would be accused of murder, and normally only guilty people were afraid of something like that.

She shook her head, tears welling up in her eyes. "But Allie, I didn't kill him. I would never kill him. Yes, it was wrong of me to lie about not knowing Paul, and I have apologized to Alec. But I would never kill anyone. You know that."

I nodded, but she clearly did not understand what was at stake. It wasn't a question of her lying. It was a question of *why* she lied. And we all knew the answer to that. "Maybe you need to talk to Alec again." I doubted it would do much good, but there was nothing I could do about this. Alec was going to continue his investigation into this case with her as his prime suspect. She had really gotten herself into a pickle.

She clasped her hands together in front of herself. It was cold out, and she wasn't wearing any gloves. "I can talk to him until I'm blue in the face, but until he finds the actual killer, I'm the one he's going to be looking at."

I leaned against my doorframe. I wanted to help her out, but I didn't see any way I could do that, not without betraying Alec, and that was one thing I would never do. "I'm sorry, Linda. I wish there was something I could do. Why did Paul come to stay at your B&B if the two of you had broken up?"

She sighed. "He didn't realize it was my B&B. It wasn't until he made the reservations that I knew who he was."

"Didn't you tell him it would be inappropriate for him to stay at your B&B since your relationship had ended? His wife certainly didn't appreciate him staying there."

She opened her mouth to say something, then closed it and sighed, looking away.

That was when I knew what she had done. "You didn't tell him it was your B&B when he called, did you? He thought he was just making reservations for the weekend at some B&B and didn't know he was making those arrangements with you."

She nodded reluctantly. "Yes. Paul Taylor was the one who got away. It may have just been an affair for him, but for me, it was everything. I loved him. He said he would leave his wife in the beginning. But of course, he did not. He left *me* instead. I thought maybe once he got here, and we did some catching up, he would feel kindly toward me. Maybe he would want to see me again. I even made Valentine's Day reservations at Antonio's in the hopes that I could convince him to stay a few days longer. I had to take Annie instead."

I bit my lower lip, trying to keep from saying the words that wanted to come out. "Oh, Linda." This was sad, and yet it was infuriating. What was she thinking?

She nodded. "I know. Believe me, I know. It was so stupid. I was hoping he had gotten a divorce and that he would be free, but when he got here and he saw me, he was angry. He said he was still happily married and intended to stay that way. My hopes were dashed, of course, but the chances of the two of us getting back together weren't great to begin with, so I accepted what he told me. I did not kill him."

I nodded. "And did you tell all of this to Alec?" He had left out some of the finer details, not that I blamed him; he had his reasons and some things he had to keep to himself.

She nodded. "Yes, I've told him everything. I gave him all the answers to all his questions, and all I can do now is hope that he understands I am not guilty."

I hoped that what she was saying was the truth. But she had already proven herself to be a liar, so I could see where Alec wouldn't believe what she told him. I nodded. "Linda, I'm afraid all we can do is wait. If somebody else killed Paul, then Alec will get to the bottom of it, and you'll be fine."

She swallowed and sniffed. "Yes. I know. I was just hoping that you could put in a good word for me."

Sighing, I said, "I've already put in a good word for you, Linda. And that's all I can do." It was hard putting in a good word for someone who had lied, but in my heart, I didn't believe she could kill anyone.

She glanced over her shoulder at her car and then back at me. "I suppose I had better let you go, then. I'm sure Alec won't appreciate me being here."

I nodded. "I don't think he will."

"Goodbye then, Allie," she said, then trudged back through the snow to her car sitting in the driveway.

"Linda!" I called after her. She turned to look at me. "Did Deanna Taylor know about the affair when it first happened?" She said she had found love letters last year, but was it true?

She shook her head. "No. Not that I'm aware of. Why?"

"I just wondered. Goodbye." I closed the door.

My heart went out to Linda. She had made some terrible mistakes—mistakes that might land her in jail. But she had to be telling the truth about not killing Paul. Or at least, I thought chances were very good that she was.

Deanna had described Paul as someone who insisted on doing what was right under any circumstances. Discovering his affair must have been a jolt to her beliefs. It undermined his commitment to always doing what was right. Was Deanna truly unaware that Linda was the B&B's owner before the blow up at Stan's Crab Shack the previous day? It's possible that upon realizing he had accidentally reserved a room with his ex-lover, Paul might have told Deanna about it in a misguided attempt at transparency. Deanna had every reason to leave him after discovering the affair, and now he was staying the weekend in the romantic B&B that his former lover owned. And did Deanna come to Maine the night before Paul's murder because she suspected the affair had reignited and wanted to catch him red-handed? If so, they might have had a confrontation over his stay at the B&B, which could have tragically led to Deanna stabbing him. I had told Alec about the video Alicia had shown me on Deanna's social media page. Maybe her errands consisted of killing her husband.

Whoever had killed Paul had to know what room he was staying in, otherwise they would have woken up the other guests looking for him. Linda named her rooms after flowers, and I had seen the name plate when I went to see what Annie was screaming about. It was the petunia room.

CHAPTER 17

Lucy took a deep breath, her eyes trained on me. "That's crazy," she finally said. She took a sip of her coffee, trying to take in the tale I had just told her.

I nodded. "It certainly was. I just don't understand Linda behaving that way. The first thing she should have done when Paul booked a room was to tell him who she was."

"And he didn't recognize her voice? I mean, he phoned in the reservation?"

"She didn't say specifically, but by the way she talked, it sounded like it. It's not like she's great with technology. She doesn't even have a website for her B&B. So Alec has his eye on her, and even though she lied, I'm having a hard time believing she could commit murder." I felt bad for Linda. If she didn't kill Paul, she had really made a mess of things by not telling the truth.

"It's a pure shame." She looked back over her shoulder at the corner table, but Mr. Winters wasn't there. "I guess it's a little late for Mr. Winters. He's probably already gone home."

I nodded and took a bite of my blueberry scone. "I think so."

She leaned forward and was just about to say something when the front door opened, and Alicia Taylor walked in. She waved at us, and we waved back, then she headed to the front counter to place an order. We both studied her in silence for a few minutes and when she had paid for her coffee, she turned and headed in our direction.

"Good morning, Allie; good morning, Lucy. Oh, it's going to be noon pretty soon, isn't it?" She chuckled and sat down at our table without asking. "It's still morning, though. How are you ladies today? You should come into the craft shop because we are having a 50% off sale for all our Valentine's Day crafts."

"Oh, that sounds fun," Lucy said. "I'm such a procrastinator. I should really buy my Valentine's Day crafts now, so maybe I'll get them done by next Valentine's Day." She chuckled.

Alicia laughed. "Now that's thinking ahead." She turned to me. "Allie, how are you? I was so happy to hear that Alec made an arrest in Paul's murder case."

I nearly choked on the scone in my mouth. I swallowed it and looked at her. "What do you mean?"

She leaned forward. "What? You didn't know? I heard Alec arrested Linda Greenwood for murdering Paul. I would have thought Alec would have told you that."

I stared at her, stunned. Had Alec found fresh evidence this morning and acted on it? Of course, I wouldn't expect him to call me and tell me first, but I sort of expected a text of some sort if he had made an arrest. I shook my head slowly. "No, I didn't know that. He left early this morning and I haven't talked to him since."

Lucy's eyes were wide. "Wow. I wasn't expecting to hear that."

Alicia nodded, grinning. "Isn't it just the most wonderful news? Now everyone can rest safely, knowing that the killer is behind bars. Honestly, I was a little surprised when I heard the news, but you never know what people are up to in their private lives. Linda Greenwood—a killer. Who knew?"

I nodded numbly. "Are you certain about that? That he made an arrest? Who did you hear it from?"

Rumors flew in this town sometimes, and it had me wondering.

She leaned in. "I heard Deanna and Linda had a fight at Stan's Crab Shack yesterday, and then Alec had to arrest her. Apparently, Linda and Paul had an affair years ago, and Deanna recently found out about it. Can you imagine? I don't know what anyone would ever see in Paul." She rolled her eyes and then went back to grinning. "But all's well that ends well. The killer is in jail, and that's the important thing."

I shook my head. "Well, I hate to break the news to you, but Linda wasn't arrested yesterday."

Alicia looked confused. "What do you mean?"

"I mean, I was there with Alec at Stan's Crab Shack. Linda went down to the station with him for questioning, but he didn't arrest her."

Her cheeks flushed pink. "What do you mean? Why wouldn't he arrest her? I heard she lied about everything. When Paul's body was found, she told your husband that she didn't even know him other than he was staying at her B&B. She's a killer. Why wouldn't he arrest her?"

What Mr. Winters had told me he found out from Daisy Taylor's neighbor, Lavonne, came to mind as I gazed at her. "Well, having an affair with someone isn't the same as murdering them."

She shook her head slowly. "Of course not. But

honestly, she has to be the killer. Who else would do it? She was right there in the B&B with him when he was killed."

I nodded. "Yes, but she doesn't have a motive to kill him. Honestly, people don't just run around murdering people without some sort of motive."

Her mouth dropped open for a moment. "But she was right there when he was murdered. And how would someone be able to slip into the B&B late at night like that? It had to be an inside job." She looked at Lucy and then back at me.

"Maybe Paul let the killer in unknowingly," Lucy said. "Just because the B&B is locked at night doesn't mean that somebody couldn't have let them in."

I nodded. "That's right. That's an excellent point, Lucy. Paul may have gotten a phone call late at night, and the killer may have met them there, and he let them in, not realizing what they were about to do. So that, of course, means that he knew the killer." I gazed at her.

"That means that he had to have known them *very* well," Lucy pointed out.

I nodded. "You're exactly right. That late at night, it would have had to have been somebody he knew *very* well. Maybe somebody that he flirted with at some time." I kept my eyes on her.

Alicia stared at me and blinked. "What do you mean? Flirted with him?"

I shrugged. "Maybe he thought his killer had an interest in him. Maybe there was a reason he chose to stay at a romantic B&B the weekend before Valentine's Day instead of staying at a motel in Bangor. Bangor isn't that far away, and whatever business he had here in town, he could have just driven here from a motel to attend to."

Lucy nodded. "I think you're right, Allie. I think he thought his killer had a romantic interest in him. Nobody stays at a romantic B&B the weekend before Valentine's Day without having romance on their mind."

"You're exactly right, Lucy. Nobody does that." I turned back to Alicia. "And certainly, the killer must have thought they were going to get something out of meeting with him at a romantic B&B. Say, a larger inheritance? Maybe they would lead him on a little."

"You're exactly right, Allie. It had to have happened that way," Lucy agreed.

She looked at Lucy and then back at me again. Slowly, she shook her head. "What do you mean? Who would think that?"

I didn't know if the girl was just dense or if she was still trying to pretend that she was innocent, but she was annoying me now. "Think about it, Alicia.

Who all stood to receive a portion of the inheritance from Daisy's death?"

She slowly raised her cup and took a sip. "I don't know what the two of you are talking about. Are you talking about me? That doesn't make any sense. Tell me, are you talking about me?"

I nodded. "We are talking about you." I'll admit it. For a moment, her innocent act made me doubt what I had just put together. But she had to be the killer.

She gasped. "Oh, you are out of your minds! There's no way I would murder anybody. Look at me, I am petite, only 5'1" tall. I couldn't do that. I don't have the strength to kill anyone."

"You're in your mid-twenties, and you look like you're fit. I think you would have absolutely no problem stabbing a man who was in his early sixties." I stared at her, waiting to see what else she would say. I hoped I wasn't making a mistake, but I was almost certain I wasn't.

She shook her head. "I don't know what's gotten into the two of you." She slowly stood up and took another sip of her coffee. "You both have lost your minds." She suddenly laughed, a harsh, hollow sound. "I'm going to call your husband. I'm going to tell him you're making false accusations. Do you think he's going to be happy with you when he finds out you've been interfering in his case?"

I smiled. "You go ahead and do that." She knew she was caught.

She spun around and stormed out of the coffee shop. Everyone in the coffee shop was looking at us, but I didn't care. Let them spread this around if they wanted to.

Lucy and I were on our feet, following her, and I hit dial on my phone. We were out in the parking lot when Alec answered, and I quickly explained what had just happened and that it was Alicia who had murdered Paul.

"I'll be right there," he said.

Alicia jumped into her car and tried to start it, but the engine sputtered and wouldn't catch. It was a bad time to have battery trouble.

CHAPTER 18

"Good evening, little lady," Alec said, leaning over and kissing the top of Lilly's head while I held her in my arms. "What are you doing up so late?" He kissed me next.

I smiled. "She couldn't sleep, so we got up to watch a little television while we waited for you to come home." It was the weekend, and Lilly was staying the night with us. She usually slept through the night, but maybe it was the fact that she knew Alec wasn't home yet that had her awake.

He sat down on the couch beside me and laid his head on my shoulder. I switched Lilly to my other arm so she could see him. "I am so tired."

"I bet you are. So what happened?" I needed the details.

"Alicia wanted to leave Jordan, and she decided that the inheritance Daisy left her just wasn't enough. She went after Paul to try to get more money from him."

"I'm surprised that Daisy left Alicia an inheritance that was separate from Jordan's. I would have thought there would have been only one portion of the inheritance and it would have gone to Jordan, or at the very least, to the two of them together."

He nodded. "Yeah, I'm surprised about that, too. But Alicia thought she could sweet-talk Paul into giving her a larger portion of it, even though the will stipulated how much she was supposed to get."

I shook my head. "Why didn't Paul just tell her that was all she was going to get and leave it at that? Why even entertain her request?" Lilly reached out her hands to Alec, and he took her from me.

"Look at you. You couldn't sleep because your granddad wasn't here, right?"

I yawned. "That about sums it up."

He kissed her on top of the head again and looked at me. "Alicia was sweet to Paul and flirted with him, and I guess he thought he was going to get somewhere with her. Why tell her she wasn't going to get more money out of it?"

I snorted. "He was nearly forty years older than she is. What on earth was he thinking?"

He nodded. "Some men just don't understand logistics. She was young and cute, and he was, well, older than her."

"So that's the real reason he booked a room at the B&B? He thought Alicia would be visiting him, and apparently she did, but not for the reasons he thought."

He sighed. "Yes, he thought he was going on a romantic getaway. Alicia visited him all right, and she gave him something he wasn't expecting."

I snorted. "I would love to have been a fly on the wall when he showed up at the B&B and realized that Linda owned it. Puts a damper on his romantic plans for a new lover when his former mistress is hovering nearby."

He chuckled. "Don't you know that had to have been the shock of his life? Linda had probably never even crossed his mind for years, and yet here she was running the romantic B&B that he planned to use for an affair with a young woman."

I smiled. What on earth was he thinking? "So, did Alicia plan to kill him that night, or did something else happen?"

"She said she brought the knife just in case, because she had no plans of carrying through with anything romantic and she might need to defend herself. Paul thought he was going to be in for some romance. But she just wanted to talk about money. She says things got physical, and she did have to defend herself."

I looked at him. "Are you kidding me? She's going to try to get off on self-defense, isn't she?"

He nodded. "Oh, yes. She's definitely going to try to get off on self-defense, and it will be up to a judge and jury to decide whether or not they believe her. I certainly do not."

I shook my head. "It takes all kinds. Poor Jordan. I bet he was in for the shock of his life, too. Hearing about this must have been devastating."

He nodded. "She called him from jail. It was ugly."

"So no one heard her stab him. And she hid the knife in the neighbor's bushes?"

He nodded. "He didn't see it coming, so there was no time to scream. She had parked several blocks away in case someone saw her car, ditching the knife beneath the snow under the bushes, and intending to retrieve it later. She never did though because she was afraid someone might see her, so she decided to leave it since she was wearing gloves when she handled it and there wouldn't be any fingerprints anyway."

I stretched and groaned. I was tired and needed to get some sleep. "Well, at least Linda wasn't guilty of murder. I'm glad about that."

He nodded. "Me too. Even though she made an excellent suspect, I really didn't want to see her go to prison for the rest of her life."

I turned and looked at Lilly. Her eyes were closed. "I think Lilly might be ready to go back to bed," I whispered.

He nodded and rested his cheek on the top of her head. "Let's give her a few more minutes to make sure she's good and ready."

I nodded and sank down onto the couch.

Valentine's Day is supposed to be a happy day for lovers, but sometimes it's a sordid day for murderers. Thankfully, Linda would be free to continue running her romantic B&B, and that was how things should be.

The end

SIGN up to receive my newsletter for updates on new releases and sales:

https://www.subscribepage.com/kathleen-suzette

Follow me on Facebook:

https://www.facebook.com/Kathleen-Suzette-Kate-Bell-authors-759206390932120

BOOKS BY KATHLEEN SUZETTE:

A PUMPKIN HOLLOW CANDY STORE MYSTERY

Treats, Tricks, and Trespassing
Gumdrops, Ghosts, and Graveyards
Confections, Clues, and Chocolate

A FRESHLY BAKED COZY MYSTERY SERIES

Apple Pie a la Murder
Trick or Treat and Murder
Thankfully Dead
Candy Cane Killer
Ice Cold Murder
Love is Murder
Strawberry Surprise Killer
Plum Dead
Red, White, and Blue Murder
Mummy Pie Murder
Wedding Bell Blunders
In a Jam
Tarts and Terror
Fall for Murder
Web of Deceit

Silenced Santa
New Year, New Murder
Murder Supreme
Peach of a Murder
Sweet Tea and Terror
Die for Pie
Gnome for Halloween
Christmas Cake Caper
Valentine Villainy
Cupcakes and Beaches
Cinnamon Roll Secrets
Pumpkin Pie Peril
Dipped in Murder
A Pinch of Homicide
Layered Lies

A COOKIE'S CREAMERY MYSTERY

Ice Cream, You Scream
Murder with a Cherry on top
Murderous 4th of July
Murder at the Shore
Merry Murder
A Scoop of Trouble
Lethal Lemon Sherbet

A LEMON CREEK MYSTERY

Murder at the Ranch
The Art of Murder
Body on the Boat

A Pumpkin Hollow Mystery Series

Candy Coated Murder
Murderously Sweet
Chocolate Covered Murder
Death and Sweets
Sugared Demise
Confectionately Dead
Hard Candy and a Killer
Candy Kisses and a Killer
Terminal Taffy

A LEMON CREEK MYSTERY

Fudgy Fatality
Truffled Murder
Caramel Murder
Peppermint Fudge Killer
Chocolate Heart Killer
Strawberry Creams and Death
Pumpkin Spice Lies
Sweetly Dead
Deadly Valentine
Death and a Peppermint Patty
Sugar, Spice, and Murder
Candy Crushed
Trick or Treat
Frightfully Dead
Candied Murder
Christmas Calamity

A RAINEY DAYE COZY MYSTERY SERIES

Clam Chowder and a Murder
A Short Stack and a Murder
Cherry Pie and a Murder
Barbecue and a Murder
Birthday Cake and a Murder
Hot Cider and a Murder
Roast Turkey and a Murder
Gingerbread and a Murder
Fish Fry and a Murder
Cupcakes and a Murder
Lemon Pie and a Murder
Pasta and a Murder
Chocolate Cake and a Murder
Pumpkin Spice Donuts and a Murder

A RAINEY DAYE COZY MYSTERY SERIES

Christmas Cookies and a Murder
Lollipops and a Murder
Picnic and a Murder
Wedding Cake and a Murder

Printed in Great Britain
by Amazon